CONTENTS

Title Page	2
One	5
Two	10
Three	14
Four	21
Five	27
Six	35
Seven	41
Eight	52
Nine	62
Ten	68
Eleven	77
Twelve	87
Thirteen	96
Fourteen	102
Fifteen	107
Sixteen	114
Seventeen	118
Eighteen	126
Nineteen	130
Twenty	136

Twenty-one	141
Twenty-two	149
Twenty-three	160
Twenty-four	164
Twenty-five	171
Twenty-six	183
Twenty-seven	186
Twenty-eight	193
Twenty-nine	201
Thirty	207
Thirty-one	212
Books In This Series	215
Books By This Author	217

WHO KILLED VIVIEN MORSE?

By Diana J Febry

All rights reserved

Names, characters and incidents depicted in this book are products of the author's imagination or are used fictitiously. Any resemblance to actual events, locales, organizations, or persons, living or dead, is entirely coincidental and beyond the intent of the author or the publisher.

No part of this book may be reproduced or transmitted in any form or by any means, electronic or mechanical, including photocopying, recording, or by any information storage and retrieval system, without permission in writing from the publisher.

Cover Art – Bigstock.com
Cover Design – Diana J Febry

Copyright © 2016 by Diana J Febry

ONE

Impeccably dressed in designer trousers, shirt and tie and blazer, DCI Peter Hatherall dashed through a torrential downpour to the station door. Turning forty had come as a horrible surprise for him. In his mid-forties, he resented having to work even harder to maintain his figure and boyish looks. With a younger second wife, thoughts about taking greater care of his health flitted into his mind on a regular basis.

Watching his friends' hairlines recede at an alarming rate, he'd become irrationally proud of his thick dark hair. Becoming a regular at the local barber shop was an easier option than looking closely at his diet or joining a gym. Running a hand through his fringe and blinking the rain from his eyes, he turned left into the reception. "Sykes, there's a car parked in my space again."

Alfred Sykes, the desk sergeant of many years, looked up from the ledger in front of him and scratched his bushy grey sideburns. "It's going to be one of those mornings for you, sir," he said with a twinkle in his eye. "I'll look into it for you. You've got an early morning visitor. Edith Pitman has been waiting to see you. She's just popped to the restroom." His bulky frame heaved up and down as he gave a hearty laugh. "Good luck with that one."

Peter turned sharply to leave. "Forget the car. You haven't seen me."

He was only inches from the door and freedom when Edith, dressed in a wax jacket, tweed skirt and wellington boots, bustled into the room. "Ah, DCI Hatherall! Were you looking for me?"

Smarting at the look of merriment on Sykes' face, Peter said, "Mrs Pitman. How lovely to see you."

"Well, we'll see about that. I'd like to have an urgent word with you about an unsavoury character that has been lurking about our neighbourhood."

With a forced smile, Peter held the door open. "Come through here. You know your way to the interview rooms." He narrowed his eyes to slits as he passed Sykes, who immediately busied himself with the contents of a ledger on the counter.

Edith sat upright in a chair and declined a cup of coffee. She ran her index finger along the desk and examined her fingertip closely before rubbing the speck of dust away with her thumb.

Peter pulled a pad towards him and picked up a pen to avoid meeting her accusatory stare. "Let's get down to business. How can we help you today?"

"I've come to advise you about the suspicious behaviour of a stranger to the area in Lower Woods. I would like to be able to inform the community watch group next Wednesday precisely what you are going to do about this man?"

"How is he acting suspiciously?" Peter asked, without looking up.

"I came across him the other day in the woods dressed in Druid robes, clearly searching for something in the undergrowth. When I asked him what he was doing, he claimed he was walking his dog. He had a guilty look written all over his face, so I asked him what he was doing poking about in the long grass with his stick. And do you know what he said?"

Peter looked up blankly at her earnest face. The sinews in her neck were taut and stringy, reminding him of a tortoise. "Surprise me."

"Looking for mushrooms! Mushrooms, I tell you."

Peter rubbed his neck and tried to dislodge the image of a tortoise lumbering through long grass, with Edith's face. "Did he have a dog with him?"

"Well yes," Edith admitted. "But that is hardly the point. He was wearing open-toed sandals and a dress. Who exercises their dog dressed like that in this weather? His toes were filthy."

Peter put his pen down and leaned back in his chair. "A little odd admittedly, but hardly a crime I could arrest him for."

Edith's nose pinched in anger. "But that's not good enough! Questions need to be asked." She stabbed the pad with her forefinger. "What is he doing here? There are young, impressionable minds in the village that need protecting."

"These minds would belong to the 'little blighters' who ride their bicycles on the pavement and nearly knocked you down last week?"

"Among others, yes. Already allowed to run wild by their parents. I'd hate to think what may happen if they came across this person alone in the woods."

"Heaven forbid," Peter said, starting to stand.

"One hears such terrible stories. Here's your opportunity to act decisively and avoid a tragedy."

"Thank you for your time, Mrs Pitman. We'll keep an eye out for this man, but there isn't really anything I can do about his fashion sense and footwear."

"But there's more, DCI Hatherall."

Peter wearily dropped his weight back into the chair. "Go on."

"My good friend, Mandy Lisle, caught him peering into her cottage window. It gave her quite a fright as you can imagine. With her nerves as they are, I'm surprised it didn't bring on one of her turns. It's not right. A man walking about in a dress, trampling through gardens to look into people's windows."

"I agree with you there. I'll arrange for someone to pay Miss Lisle a visit to obtain a full report about the incident." Swivelling the notepad round to face Edith and handing her a pen, he added, "Could you jot her address down?" Once she'd finished writing, he asked, "Do you have any idea where this Druid is staying in the area?"

Handing the notepad back, Edith replied, "From the circumstances, I deduce he is a vagrant trying to find a cottage to force himself into. Until he does so, he's probably sleeping rough. In my opinion, he poses a serious threat to us all. Hardly the sort of person we want around here. I'm quite sure the earl wouldn't be happy to know someone is creeping around his estate and sleeping in his barns. Oh, and another thing. Yesterday when I was in the post office collecting my pension, Iris from number seven said she had seen him talking to that brazen hussy Gladys Jones. Since she's been forced out of the big house, she's not so high and mighty anymore, I can tell you. As for that brother of hers..."

Peter stood and raised his hand for Edith to stop. "Okay, leave the matter with me, and I'll look into it." He opened the door to the interview room to usher her out.

Pulling a headscarf from her handbag and tying it over her head, Edith said, "So what should I tell the community watch group on Wednesday? What are you going to do about the problem?"

"I suggest you reassure the group that we are looking into the matter. I'll have a better idea once we've spoken to Miss Lisle. Come this way, and I'll show you out."

In the corridor, Edith continued to grumble. "It isn't right. Grown men wearing dresses and conjuring up mumbo jumbo while talking to trees." Pulling up the zip of her coat to her chin, she said, "Sex. That's what's behind it all. You mark my words. Sex and dancing naked in the woods. That's what it will all lead to."

"I thought he was wearing a dress?"

"For now. Men in dresses! It's not right, I tell you."

Holding the front door open, Peter said, "I don't think your vicar would be happy to be described as wearing a dress."

"That's completely different. It's a cassock, and he wears sensible shoes underneath."

Sighing, Peter said, "Goodbye, Mrs Pitman. A pleasure as always, but could I give you some advice? It would be better if you didn't accost strange men in the woods. It could be dangerous."

"Phooey! I pity the man who tries to trifle with me. Good day."

Under his breath, Peter said, "So do I." He popped his head into the reception. "Sykes, have you seen a Druid priest wandering about the area recently?"

"Aye," Sykes nodded his head. "Assuming there is only the one, I bumped into him in The Squire Inn when I took the missus out for her birthday. Seemed a harmless enough chap. Just a bit potty."

"He'll fit in well around here then."

"Aye, happen he will. I've had the car moved from your space while you were occupied."

"Thanks," Peter replied, and made his way up the stairs to his office, bumping into Detective Constable Eddie Jordon in the corridor. "Ah Jordon, I was going to come and find you." He handed him the sheet of paper and said, "Can you pay this lady a visit today? There's been a complaint about a Druid priest of all things peering into her cottage window. I don't suppose you've seen one wandering about the area?"

"No, afraid not, sir."

"Well, let me know how you get on." Peter walked away quickly, relieved to have passed on the request to someone else.

As soon as he opened the door to his office, DI Fiona Williams handed him a coffee. "Where've you been? We've just had an urgent call. The body of a woman has been discovered this morning by a dog walker out in Silver Lady Woods."

Peter closed his eyes, trying to eradicate the conversation with Mrs Pitman from his mind so he could think straight. "I take it she's dead?"

"I'm afraid so. No other details other than we're needed out there so they can move the body."

"Well if she's dead, another couple of minutes' delay while I finish my coffee won't make any difference will it?"

TWO

Peter gave Detective Constable Phil Humphries a grim nod before holding up the crime tape for Fiona and following her down the steep bank covered in a thick layer of fallen autumn leaves. The air was still and cloying, weighed down and immobilised by the moisture of the deep fog. The cold damp attached itself to everything in its wake, adding another layer of dreariness to an already drab day. The last few crinkled leaves that clung valiantly to the branches drooped under the weight of the atmosphere as they tried to delay joining the mulch of fallen leaves underfoot.

Fiona slipped halfway down the bank, hitting her shoulder on a tree trunk that stopped her fall. Despite the dank air smothering the thud of the impact, Alex Stokes, the medical examiner, looked up abruptly from where he was kneeling, drawing more attention to her clumsy entrance. "Careful, for goodness sake. This is a crime scene." The photographer and several other officers clad in white overalls working in the background looked over and away again.

Annoyance showed in Stokes' angular bird-like facial features. Ignoring Fiona, he gave Peter a curt nod of acknowledgement before returning his attention to his work.

Detective Constable James Smith smiled at Fiona and offered his hand. "Careful, it's really slippery just here."

Fiona returned the smile but refused the offer of help. She took small steps towards him, determined not to lose her footing again. Peter winked from behind her and asked, "Were you the first on the scene?"

DC Smith, who stood a head above Peter, replied, "Pretty much. She was found this morning at about six thirty by a dog walker called Kathy Hooper. It was drizzling with rain earlier, and she was impatient to get home into the dry to get ready for work. Detective Sergeant Ward took her home, but I've got all the details."

Alex Stokes interrupted them. "Morning Peter. Fiona," he said, nodding to them both in turn. "There's not much more I can do here except catch pneumonia. I'll confirm all the details in my report, but in my opinion, she was attacked early yesterday evening. Rigour mortis is already established so she would have been killed in this situ at nine o'clock at the latest. Probably a little earlier. She sustained severe head injuries, and my best guess at this stage was she was hit several times with a blunt object. From the splinters of wood embedded in her hair, possibly by something like a fallen branch. Sexual assault is a low probability." With a wide smile showing crooked teeth he added, "Would you like to take a closer look before she is moved?"

Returning a stiff smile, Peter replied, "I'll take a quick look before I leave," glancing towards the photographer and back again. "I'm sure we'll have a full set of photographs. Can you tell me anything else about the victim at this stage?"

"Smartly dressed. Professional office wear, I'd say," Alex said. "Late twenties to early thirties."

"What type of shoes was she wearing?" Peter said, walking the few steps to where the body lay, sprawled face down in the mud as if she had slipped like Fiona had earlier.

Alex crouched by the woman's feet. One shoe was securely in place, the other had fallen off a few inches away. "Heels and the mud on the soles along with the positioning of her body suggests she walked down here to her death."

"Sir," Smith said. "Sorry to butt in, but Humphries thinks he knows her. If he's right, then I've seen her around the courts as well. We think she's a local social worker who works mostly with young offenders."

"Thank you," Peter said, dismissing Alex and turning his attention to James. "How much do you know about her?"

"Assuming we're correct, her name was Vivien Morse. I'm not totally sure, but Humphries had a better look and knew her more than me, so he probably is the best person to ask." He rolled his eyes before adding, "Humphries got along with her, but she wasn't terribly popular with the rest of us."

"How come?"

"She got more than a few kids off the hook with her bleeding-heart tales. I think she possibly believed all their hard luck stories and their promises never to be so naughty again." He shook his head. "Probably one of those little buggers who should have been put away, did this."

"It's too early for such assumptions," Peter said. "How well did Humphries know her?"

"You didn't hear this from me, but she recently split with her husband and Humphries had designs on her. I don't think he got very far, though."

Fiona touched Peter's arm to get his attention and said, "I'll go and find him," before turning to make her way back up to the top of the bank.

Peter cast his eye over the SOCO team picking over the scene. "Has anyone found her handbag?"

"Not yet. She doesn't appear to have put up much of a fight. Not here anyway. There's nothing at all to indicate a struggle and Stokes said she hadn't been dragged down here."

Peter tapped his lips with his index finger deep in thought. "An odd place for someone dressed for the office to be wandering about, especially considering the wet weather last night. Although, if I remember right, it did clear up for a few hours about tea time."

"Evidence suggests she received the blows to her head here and it also indicates she came down here willingly, despite being inappropriately dressed."

"No chance she could have been half-carried here while semi-unconscious? From a car parked over there perhaps?" Peter asked, looking towards where he'd left his own car.

James shook his head and pointed in the opposite direction. "Unless someone else was walking around here in stilettos last night, she came from over there under her own steam. With the ground so saturated it's hard to identify any other footprints, but the spikes from her high heels have left imprints."

Peter looked into the fuzzy gloom as the persistent drizzle turned to rain. "The fog is getting worse. Any idea what is up that way?"

"Haven't got that far yet."

"Any sign of her car?"

"I'll get on to it straight away, sir," James replied.

"Keep me posted. I don't see the point of us all standing around here getting wet. I'll go and speak to the dog walker and her husband. Careful you don't slip!"

With rain dripping from his nose, James said, "Think of us while you're having a nice cup of tea in the dry."

THREE

A cold wind picked up, driving the persistent rain into Peter's face as climbed the bank. At the top, he stepped over a large brown puddle where rainfall had mixed with runoff from the adjacent ploughed fields. Water dripped from him as he climbed into the car. Fiona was in the passenger seat already logged on to her laptop.

Running a hand through his wet hair, Peter asked, "Was Humphries able to confirm the woman was this Vivien Morse?"

Without looking up from the screen, Fiona replied, "Yes. You might want to go easy on him. He had quite a soft spot for her and is very upset."

"Humphries? That's a turn up for the book. I wasn't previously aware he even had a softer side. The one and only time I've seen him express emotion was over an England rugby game," Peter said, peering out the misted-up window at the massive hunk of Detective Constable Humphries. He started the car engine and turned the screen fan on full blast and waited for the windscreen to clear. "How well did he know her?"

"Not as well as he would have liked. She only recently separated from her husband and told him she needed a friend but wasn't ready for new commitments. She's divorcing her husband for abusive behaviour, and you'll love this."

"Go on. Don't keep me in suspense."

"There's a history of domestic violence going back a couple of years. Concerned neighbours contacted us several times to intervene, but Vivien always refused to press charges. However, she obtained an injunction against him a few weeks ago after he attacked her and one of her friends outside a nightclub in town. I've looked up his present address. It's in Sapperton."

The car tyres sent up a spray of brown sludge that ran down the side windows as Peter drove out of the shallow pothole he'd parked in to avoid blocking the narrow lane. "Good chance this is a straightforward domestic then, but we'll bring him in officially to give a formal identification. He's probably on his way to work this time of day. Do you know if someone has contacted him?"

"Without a definite ID, I doubt it. I could ring him now?"

"Contact DS Abbie Ward first to tell her we're going to visit the husband and we'll speak to the dog walker later." Switching the windscreen wipers to maximum speed as heavy rain battered the car, he said, "I'm so fed up with this weather."

Fiona twisted towards him in her seat. "You sound generally fed up this morning about everything."

"Weary more than anything." Taking a sharp right turn onto a single-track lane that twisted and turned up Lordsworth Hill, he swore at the sight of a tractor pulling a trailer load of manure up ahead of them. "Damn! I should have taken the longer route to the main road. That's going to be crawling along at zero miles an hour by the time it reaches the top."

"He might turn off before," Fiona said, brightly.

"I hope he does," Peter replied, drumming his fingers on the steering wheel. "Have you called Ward yet?"

A brief call told Fiona the witness had already left for work but had agreed to visit the station as soon as her shift finished to give a formal statement. Before she disconnected the call, Peter indicated he wanted a word with Abbie. "DCI Hatherall here. You're telling me she just calmly got dressed for work and went in? Not distressed or freaked out by discovering a dead body?" He listened for a while before handing the phone back to Fiona. "Most odd for her to be so unconcerned."

"Delayed shock?" Fiona suggested. "What does she do for a living?"

"A community nurse. She told Ward she does a lot of palliative care so isn't bothered by the sight of dead bodies, but I still find it strange. There's a world of difference between an old person dying peacefully in their bed and the sudden shock of coming across the body of a young woman who has been brutally attacked."

"I agree, but it takes all sorts, and sadly young people fall victim to fatal conditions as well. How do you think Stokes would react if he came across something similar? It's not like the body was mutilated or a particularly gruesome sight."

"That cold fish is hardly representative of the rest of the population. Regardless of the nature of her job, I'd expect some sort of emotional response. I want to make sure we see her this afternoon." Changing gear as the tractor's progress up the hill slowed, Peter said, "Give the victim's husband a ring to see if he is at home. I wouldn't mind being able to speak to him before he's assigned a Family Liaison Officer."

Fiona dialled the number but received no reply. "He's not answering."

"It won't do any harm to swing by his home on the off chance he's decided not to go into work today. Assuming, of course, he has a job," Peter said.

Fiona's quip of, "You haven't even met him yet," was met with a grunt, so she settled back in her seat and turned her attention to the laptop.

Out of the silence, Peter said, "Sorry I'm not in the best of moods today."

"I had noticed."

"And making polite conversation to a guy who used his wife as a punch bag and very likely went too far last night isn't going to improve it," Peter said.

"You weren't exactly cheery first thing this morning before you heard about the case."

"You didn't have the pleasure of that old battle axe Edith Pitman first thing this morning complaining about someone in sandals walking their dog. As if we've nothing else to do with our time other than interview people she's decided to take a dislike to. And if someone hadn't taken my car space this morning, I might have avoided that particular joy. With a dead body turning up, I know who those busybodies will be holding to blame."

"It is something worth considering. I wouldn't walk around in sandals in this weather," Fiona joked.

"If you're happy to jump to the same small-minded assumptions, maybe you could take my place and liaise with the neighbourhood watch group. You might even enjoy their meetings."

Fiona bit her tongue and gave her laptop her full attention. She looked up when she felt the car slowing. "He's pulling over to let you pass. See, there are some thoughtful people in the world. Not everyone is so grumpy first thing in the morning."

Accelerating past and raising a hand in thanks to the tractor driver, Peter said, "Don't go to the other extreme and become all new wave and hippy on me. I get enough of that from my daughter Amelia. Sally isn't much better. Trying to find herself all the time, whatever that means. I don't have to go searching for myself. I'm exactly where I left myself the night before, when I wake up in the morning. And my inner self isn't battling to escape so it can communicate with astral beings." At the brow of the hill, he said, "Sorry. Sorry. I shouldn't be taking my bad mood out on you. I didn't get much sleep last night."

"No worries. How come?"

Peter gave a good impression of total concentration on driving as he pulled out onto the main dual carriageway that would take them into Sapperton. With a sigh, he said, "I've no idea what is going on at home. Amelia got up at three o'clock this morning to start baking cakes. The whirring sound of food mixers at high speed woke me."

"I expect she's just worried. Starting up her own business must be very stressful," Fiona said.

"Just how stressful can baking a cake be?" Peter replied. Softening his tone, he said, "Yeah. Yeah. I know what you're getting at, and I am concerned about it being too much for her."

"How does it seem to be going so far? She sounded really excited about the prospect when I saw her a few months ago."

"Fine. She already has a few customers. I forgot you two went out clubbing together. God, that makes me feel old."

As Peter lapsed back into a grumpy silence, Fiona reached forwards and turned on the car radio. "Do you mind?" Peter shook his head, and while Fiona sat back to enjoy the music, Peter relaxed a little. After a few songs played back to back, the DJ announced a news break. The last bulletin concerned a convicted con man and cat burglar of the rich and famous called Rob Creer. He had been rushed to hospital following a brawl at Shoreham Prison. The reporter took great delight in pointing out that his cache of money rumoured to be in excess of several million pounds had never been recovered. He fell just short of inciting his listeners in the Midlands to rush out of their homes and start searching. Next came a weather girl brightly forecasting yet more wind and rain was on its way to batter the coasts and bring additional misery to areas already flooded.

"Turn it off," Peter said. "I can see the rain for myself." Once the radio was switched off, he continued, "I remember that Creer case. The guy operated all over the country. At one time he was in the frame for a spate of burglaries around here. Two years running invitees to the earl's annual hunt ball were broken into."

"What happened?"

"I can't remember exactly. It was one of DCI Jenkins' cases. Or should I say Detective Superintendent Jenkins now? Talking of which his old position should be advertised shortly."

"And?"

"And?" Peter turned and gave Fiona a surprised look. "And I expected you to be pestering me to support your application."

Averting her attention to the passenger window, Fiona replied, "I've been preoccupied recently."

"Is everything okay at home?"

"Everything is fine." Turning from the window, Fiona said, "Tell me more about this Creer case."

"As I recall, it turned out the burglaries were nothing to do with him. It was decided it must have been someone local who knew the houses would be empty."

"Did they catch him?"

"Who? The local burglar? No."

"Isn't Shoreham a high-security prison? How come a burglar ended up there?" Fiona asked.

"Because on his last break-in the house wasn't empty and Creer ended up shooting the owner. Then a few weeks later, he drove his car on purpose into a teenage girl riding a bicycle while trying to escape." Peter's mind flittered to the unsolved hit and run file he kept in his desk. Put there many years ago, when he naively believed that one day he'd find the driver who killed his school friend. "Anyway, it's hardly likely to concern us so back to concentrating on our case. We should be there any minute. Does Mr Morse have a first name and what does he do for a living?"

"Nigel, but I've no details of his employment."

Nigel Morse's house was a three bedroom, semi-detached on an older part of the Sapperton sprawling housing estate. Built in an age when one car families were the norm, each house was allotted one single garage at the rear of the property. As most adults now believed they couldn't survive without their own vehicle, the excess cars were rammed haphazardly into every possible space between the rear garages, leaving nowhere nearby for Peter to park. He finally managed to parallel-park in an impossibly small space on an adjacent street between two rusted vehicles with dents in the doors.

Nigel's address was number twenty-three Somerset Paradise. A strange name as they weren't in the county of Somerset nor was there anything of beauty to be seen.

Walking along the drab street, Peter said, "The design of this estate may make it a house burglar's paradise, but it's hardly the Promised Land to anyone else." They followed the oil-stained pavement, squeezing between cars in various states of road worthiness.

Although more spacious than the newer houses on the estate, the buildings were ugly and uniform. Row upon row of identical concrete squares stretched out as far as the eye could see. Without any side alleyways to reach the front of the properties, access from the road was through the rear garden. Running the length of the street at regular intervals wooden gates were set into the red brick, six-foot wall. Unless the house occupant was a recluse without any friends or visitors likely to call, the gate would be unlocked and held by a simple catch. In the past, whenever residents tried to protect the rear of their property by installing security devices, they found them smashed or stolen by the following morning.

Parked outside number twenty-three was a red BMW. The roof and bonnet were piled high with traffic cones and takeaway wrappers from the local fish and chip shop.

"Late night shenanigans," Peter commented.

Fiona replied, "At least somebody had a fun time last night."

As anticipated, Nigel Morse's gateway was unlocked. They left the pavement and followed the narrow path to the back door. The small strip of grass posing as a garden would never receive any sunlight due to the height of the impersonal red brick wall isolating it from the neighbouring houses on either side. Until humans grew to seven feet tall, there was no chance of a friendly chat over the garden wall in this neighbourhood.

A tiny stone patio area, just big enough to take a picnic bench, was set to the side of the back door. Sharing a relaxing evening drink would give a depressing view of red brick walls and grey rooftops stretching into the far distance.

FOUR

The white pvc door had no bell or knocker. Peter knocked loudly a few times before lifting the letterbox and shouting, "Nigel. Nigel Morse? Are you in there?"

After a short while sounds of movement could be heard and an upstairs window opened. A head poked out and shouted, "Yeah. Who wants to know?"

Peter stepped away from the door and looked up. "The police. Can you come down and let us in?"

The thud of the window being slammed shut was followed by the sound of creaking floorboards and a bolt being drawn back. The lock mechanism of the door clunked loudly, and the door crept open a few inches. "Have the little sods vandalised my car again?"

"Not as far as I'm aware," Peter replied, pushing the traffic cones from his mind. "Can we come in?"

"What's it about?"

"Your ex-wife," Peter replied. He quickly stepped forwards using his shoulder to prevent the door from slamming shut in their faces.

"I've been nowhere near the little slut, and if she says different, she's a bloody liar." Accepting he couldn't shut the door, Nigel flung it open. "So what crap has she been telling you?"

Peter stepped inside with Fiona behind him. "Do you want to get dressed first?" Nigel Morse would not find a career as an underwear model. His flabby stomach over hung the top of his boxer shorts, and his surprisingly skinny legs were pink with red blotches. His long grey chest hairs and overnight facial stubble confirmed his jet-black head of hair was out of a bottle. Sore looking acne on his upper arms battled with faded blue tattoos.

The back door led directly into a narrow kitchen area, too small to accommodate seating. Seemingly happy with his own body, Nigel scratched his belly, causing a rippling effect and replied, "Not really," and turned his back on them to flick on a kettle sitting on one of the side counters. "I am, however, going to make myself a coffee." He opened an overhead cupboard and pointedly pulled out one mug before snatching a blue envelope from the side and slipping it into a drawer.

"No sugar for either of us," Peter said. "Just milk." When Nigel reluctantly retrieved two more mugs, he added, "Who was the letter from?"

"My mother," Nigel quickly replied. "I set up a Facebook account for her and showed her how to use it, but you know what older people are like."

"You're lucky to have a mother who cares. We'll go through to the other room and make ourselves at home," Peter said, heading towards the door.

When Nigel joined them, he'd pulled on a pair of jogging bottoms and a matching blue sweatshirt. Small veins of red crisscrossed his bulging eyes as he forced a smile and handed out the mugs of coffee. "Look. About the wife. I've accepted the situation. I was a fool to let her go, but what's done is done. Much as I'd like to, I can't turn back the clocks of time, and I've no wish to make things difficult for her. It's time we all moved on and got on with our lives. But just for the record, Vivien is not my ex as the divorce hasn't come through yet."

"Take a seat," Peter said, indicating the vacant armchair. "When was the last time you saw Vivien?"

Nigel ran a hand through his tousled bed hair. "I'm sure you have it all on record."

Peter continued to look expectantly at him for a reply.

Nigel gave a heavy sigh and put his coffee mug down. "It was a stupid thing to do. I know that. It was the drink talking, but I've explained all this before. I haven't been anywhere near her since the incident in town. All contact since has been via our solicitors."

"When was the incident?" Fiona asked.

"A few weeks ago. Surely you know that?"

Peter seemed preoccupied with a series of photographs on the mantelpiece over a fake marble fireplace. Fiona waited briefly before asking, "Are you heading out for a run this morning?"

"No. Why do you ask?"

"That's a pretty snazzy tracksuit you're wearing, and the trainers by the kitchen door are top quality. I thought you might have been a serious runner?" As Nigel didn't comment, Fiona asked, "Where were you yesterday and last night?"

Nigel cast a nervous glance towards Peter who continued to ignore him before replying, "I was in Cornwall meeting with the owners of various toy shops." In response to Fiona's quizzical look, he continued to explain. "I'm a sales rep, in fact, I'm the top sales rep for Playthings." When Fiona raised her eyebrows, he blushed and quickly added, "They make soft toys. For children. Teddy bears and other stuffed animals."

"Ah!" Peter exclaimed. "That would explain the photographs."

"I'm not a... Well, you know what, if that's what you're thinking," Nigel said defensively.

Peter held out his hands in mock innocence. "I wasn't thinking anything. I just wondered if all the children in the pictures were nieces and nephews."

"I know what you were suggesting."

Determined to keep things on track Fiona interrupted the two men, "What time did you get back from Cornwall, and could you give us the names and addresses of the customers you met?"

Nigel reluctantly pulled himself from his seat to retrieve a briefcase propped against the wall near the door. He clicked open the combination lock and pulled out a wad of paperwork.

"I had a very successful day. They all gave me orders," he said, dropping the pile of order forms in Fiona's lap. Seating himself, he explained, "You can't keep those, but you can copy down the details. If you give me some contact information, I can e-mail or post copies as soon as I get into the office."

Making a note of the names and addresses and the appointment times, Fiona asked, "Where's your office?"

"Central Birstall, on King Street, next to the Burger King."

Fiona offered the invoices to Peter who was sitting to her right, but he waved them away. Leaning forwards to return them to Nigel, she said, "Thank you. Why aren't you at work this morning?"

"I'll be going in as soon as we're finished here. I work in sales, not a nine to five job. It's all performance related."

"Are you a good performer?" Peter asked.

"I've already told you. I'm the top salesperson at Playthings."

"What time did you arrive home yesterday and what did you do for the rest of the evening?" Fiona asked.

Tearing his eyes from Fiona's cleavage, Nigel fumbled in his pockets for his phone, adjusting his jogging bottoms as he did so. "I telephoned the boss about six o'clock from Membury Services to say I wouldn't be coming back to the office as I was held up in traffic. I arrived home about an hour later, had a shower and watched a bit of TV while I waited for my booked taxi to arrive. It took me to the Willy Wicket pub on the by-pass where I treated myself to a celebratory meal and a pint. I left at closing time, and as it had stopped raining, I walked home."

"Did you meet up with friends or walk home with anyone?"

"I only moved here a month or so ago, so I don't really know the locals. The landlord will confirm I ate there and I did chat to a couple of lads in the bar afterwards. I've no idea where they live or their last names, but they were called Tim and Mark." He wandered over to the fake fireplace and picked up a business card from the mantelpiece. He handed it to Fiona before sitting down.

"The taxi cab firm I used. They'll be able to give the exact time they picked me up."

Fiona slipped the card between the pages of her notepad. "And what did you do when you arrived home?"

"I went to bed…Look what's this about? You asked about Vivien earlier."

Peter reached for a framed photograph and turned it to face Nigel. "Is this a good likeness of your wife?"

"Umm. Yes, I guess. How did you know?"

Without answering, Peter asked, "How would you describe your marriage?"

"Good. It was good," Nigel replied, nodding his head as if to prove to himself and them that was a true statement.

"Your wife obviously didn't agree," Peter said with raised eyebrows.

"It was fine before all the prison nonsense, but I do accept I screwed up and ruined a good thing," Nigel replied.

"Prison thing?"

"Up north. Before we moved down here, she regularly visited prisoners. It's what destroyed our marriage. She visited the really sick-in-the-head ones. Murderers and paedophiles. Despite being the scum of the earth, they had all her sympathy as she accepted whatever excuse they gave. Abusive childhoods, poverty, lack of role models, blah, blah, blah. But when it came to me, I couldn't even leave the toilet seat up without getting the fifth degree. A pint on the way home from work and I was an alcoholic. Nag, nag, nag. I couldn't do right for doing wrong."

"Is that why you moved down here? To put a stop to her prison visits?" Peter asked.

"She saw it that way, but it was a promotion opportunity for me. I was hoping with the extra money we could think about starting a family. I guess Vivien wanted something else."

"Interesting," Peter said, standing. "I'd like more details of those prison visits at some point, but for now we need you to come with us."

Standing, Nigel nervously said, "Why? I haven't done anything."

Fiona got in quickly before Peter and said, "We believe Vivien was seriously assaulted last night. At the station, we can organise a Family Liaison Officer for you, and if you feel up to it, we do need someone to give a formal identification."

The colour drained from Nigel's face as he sank back down into the chair. "Viv? No, that's not possible. I mean. Is she in hospital? Unconscious? Yes. That's what you mean surely." He looked up with a pleading look. "She's going to be okay? Isn't she?"

FIVE

Deep in thought, Peter remained perched on the edge of the desk, tapping a marker pen in a rhythm. After he'd dismissed the small team, DS Abbie Ward had called Fiona over for a quick word. While he waited for Fiona, he stared at the few notes on the board alongside the image of Vivien Morse. Her ordinariness struck a chord somewhere deep inside. This was a woman you'd pass in the street without noticing. An insignificant nobody in the larger scale of things. Her sudden death the one newsworthy occurrence in her life that thrust her into the limelight. Peter made a silent promise to her picture to find her attacker.

He ran through in his head the duties he'd handed out. DCs James Smith and Phil Humphries were to check Nigel's alibi at the Willy Wicket. If the alibi was confirmed, they could start door to door enquiries in the tiny village of Supworth near where Vivien was discovered. DC Andrew Litten and DS Abbie were to contact the family liaison officer assigned to Vivien Morse's parents and then start to investigate her background and friends. He'd asked them to give special attention to her time as a prison visitor and whether any of the inmates she visited had been recently released.

◆ ◆ ◆

"How about we meet up tonight for a good old girlie chat?" Abbie asked Fiona. "A couple of bottles of wine and a chick flick?"

"I can't tonight; I'm going out with Julien. We're going to watch the new Star Wars movie," Fiona quickly replied. "Maybe another night."

Abbie frowned. "When I asked you to watch the film with me, you said you hated sci-fi films and hadn't bothered to watch any of the others. Why the sudden change of heart?"

Fiona shrugged. "I changed my mind. I really should be getting back." Glancing across the room, she added, "Peter looks impatient to be off."

"Have you told him about Julien yet?"

Irritated by Abbie's knowing look, Fiona said, "I think I've mentioned him. We talk about work mostly. Talking of which …"

"Tomorrow night then? At my house. You bring the wine and a film, I'll cook."

"Sure."

"And don't you dare cancel last minute like last time."

"Okay. Promise. Tomorrow night it is."

Approaching Peter, Fiona tried to not question why an event she'd normally look forward to, made her feel slightly uneasy. She pushed the sense of foreboding to the back of her mind, deciding to blame it on Abbie and her unwanted interest in her private life.

She had trouble sleeping recently, but she hadn't noticed she had dark circles under her eyes until Abbie pointed them out. Then again, maybe she hadn't had them before. Maybe it was Abbie fussing that had caused the problem in the first place. Fiona chewed her lip, trying to establish which came first, the trouble sleeping or Abbie fussing about how tired she looked.

"Ready now?" Peter said, standing in the doorway already dangling his keys.

Before they left the station, he emptied the contents of a small lunch box into the bin in the reception area. In response to Fiona's quizzical look, he said, "Sally is toying with veganism. Battle lines are set in the kitchen. On the one side sponges and icing and on the other soaked lentils and hummus."

"When does Amelia pick up the keys to her new shop?"

"Next Monday, but I fear she will continue to bring her work home."

Once in the car, Peter said, "Sally complains I'm old fashioned but talking to Nigel Morse was like stepping back in time. 'Me man, who provides and does whatever I choose; you woman who does whatever I choose. And if you think otherwise, my fists will explain the situation'."

"You think it's a straightforward domestic violence then?"

"Much as I don't like the guy, I'm not sure. If his alibi holds up, the timing would be tight and if Vivien had an injunction against him, why wander into the woods with him? It was hardly the weather last night for a chat over a picnic about the state of their marriage."

"True." Fiona wondered if this was more wishful thinking as he wanted a distraction from issues at home. "Did you notice the two new suits hanging on the back of Morse's kitchen door?"

"Vaguely."

"You didn't spot they were pretty good quality. They must have cost a fair penny."

"I guess he needs to be smart for work and sees quality suits as a good investment. Plus, he's facing a divorce. Realising he's going to be single again soon might have given him the urge to spruce himself up a bit," Peter said.

"There's quality, and then there's quality. I don't think there would have been much change from a thousand pounds."

"Really? You could tell that just by looking at them? There's some good knockoff stuff around that looks like the real thing, but you can pick it up at a fraction of the cost."

"Maybe," Fiona replied, sounding less than convinced.

"Well, just park the idea for now until we find out what sort of life assurance Vivian had."

Vivien's employers were on the third floor of a new building development overlooking Birstall Harbour. The area was considered an engineering masterpiece. The mud flats and sludge of the estuary were no more as during the first phase the water had been channelled between concrete walkways. The regimented water now lined with fancy restaurants, wine bars and upmarket boutiques, could only gently lap the uniform walls when once it had roared.

A short distance away along the riverside, the abandoned red brick factories stained by black soot that had once shaped the horizon had been demolished. In their place, modern office complexes were springing up through the cracked concrete.

At the building entrance, an automatic door silently opened on their approach. Inside, deep pile carpet softened the otherwise sterile clean lines of the minimalist design. The chrome and metal sparkled while each step on the deep pile carpet sent up wafts of chemical newness.

The receptionist's shirt had the starched worn-for-the-first-time texture. She smiled nervously as they approached her desk. At least any new start-up glitches had been already dealt with as she efficiently telephoned to advise of their arrival. Handing over their visitor badges she said, "Ms Salt will be with you shortly."

They were deciding whether to take advantage of the complimentary coffee from the machine. The extensive selection available slowed them down while the rich aroma of real ground coffee mocked their indecision.

They turned in unison at the sound of an educated voice with crystal clear clipped tones. "DCI Hatherall and Williams."

An elegant and expensively dressed woman glided towards them with an outstretched hand. "Please call me Jane. We're very relaxed and informal here." Her well-practised smile, intended to put them at ease, unnerved Fiona as she felt the woman's penetrating eyes assess her. If this was her being relaxed and casual, her professional persona must be sharp enough to take someone's eye out.

Engulfed in more than a subtle hint of perfume, they were led to a pair of lifts. The silent mechanism of the lift explained why they were caught unaware by Jane's arrival. The panel of lights gave the only indication they were moving between floors.

"We're all devastated by the news. Vivien was a highly valued member of my team. Always cheerful, she had time for everyone, whatever else was going on in her life. She is going to be missed terribly," Jane announced as the lift doors re-opened into an airy corridor. Bright splashes of colour lined the walls from a dazzling collection of abstract art. Jane continued, "I've known her a number of years and thought of her as a friend rather than an employee. I can't quite believe she's gone. It's a very upsetting time for all of us."

Her words sounded rehearsed and false and judging from her clear complexion and perfect eye makeup, Fiona doubted Jane had shed any tears over the loss. The final door opened taking them into a spacious open plan office with ten workstations.

Currently only one was in use where a man and woman, both around their late thirties huddled around a slight blond-haired woman whose face was hidden as she sobbed loudly. During their walk through the office, her cries became louder, and her work colleagues created a tighter group in their attempt to console her. The man gave Fiona a weak apologetic smile before Jane hurried them into her private office. Once inside, she pulled a colourful screen across the glass window, blocking their view of the rest of the office.

"We will want to speak to Vivien's colleagues," Peter said.

"Of course. The job is field-based, but I'll give you the full contact details of those currently out. First things first. Do you take milk and sugar in your coffee?" Jane said, heading towards a side room. Returning with mugs filled with hot steaming liquid, she continued. "This really is a most dreadful thing to happen. Considering the work we do, it shouldn't have come as a terrible surprise, but I'm afraid it has. We deal with violent home situations all the time, but we never think it could happen to one of us."

Jane wheeled her leather office chair from behind her desk to place it closer to the two chairs occupied by Peter and Fiona. "Although I knew about the problems Vivien had with her husband, I was not expecting anything quite this violent." Looking over her coffee cup after taking a sip she asked, "Do you have him in custody?"

"Do you know Nigel Morse?" Peter asked by way of a reply.

"Not particularly well. I've met him at a couple of work-related social events. I'd like to say we've exchanged the usual pleasantries, but that would be a lie. He took full advantage of the free bar and became rude and abusive. We had one very heated conversation when Vivien first transferred here. I made it clear to him that while we had vaguely known each other during our university days, I did not wish him to contact me privately again."

"You knew each other before?"

"I studied the same university course as Vivien, and we shared a hall of residence in our first year. That was the year the two of them met, and I did go out a few times with them on double dates. I'm afraid at the time I had a string of different boyfriends, none of them lasting longer than a couple of months. Even then Nigel was boorish and arrogant and as tight as a tart's handbag."

Jane paused to sip from her coffee. "He's the type who chooses the cheapest items on the menu when you go for a meal and then insists on pulling out a calculator to ensure everyone pays the exact amount. When I moved out in my second year into rented accommodation, I found new friends and lost track of them. I had a little more contact with Vivien in my third year when we were partnered up as volunteer prison visitors to gain some practical experience. I think that really showed up our different areas of expertise."

"How do you mean?"

"She really took to the experience and went on about how worthwhile the visits were in terms of her understanding of people who needed her help. She genuinely believed her visits could make a difference. I admit it is a part of the job I don't relish. I'm afraid I view prison visits as something to be endured on occasion and find the places unsettling and depressing. Certainly not something I'd choose to do voluntarily in my free time. But then, as I'm sure you'll discover, Vivien was a very generous, giving soul."

"And the heated discussion? What was that about?" Peter asked.

"He had the audacity to say he was uncomfortable about Vivien being assigned male clients and expected me to do something about it. Honestly! I recall I was rather blunt and told him to sort out his insecurity issues. I may have been a little ruder than that, but that was the gist of my advice. Although this unit is lucky to be located in these plush new offices, don't let that fool you. We remain as understaffed and underpaid as ever." Shaking her head, Jane added, "As if I'd have time to reassign workloads on that basis. Ridiculous little man. He had issues with her working full-stop. That's why she was only part-time. She told me once he was so tight with money she'd starve and live on baked beans otherwise and yet he put pressure on her to start a family. The odious jerk."

"Okay, we get the picture with her husband. Generally, are relationships between clients and employees ever an issue?"

"We discuss quite personal matters with vulnerable people, many of whom have mental health problems. We are trained to be totally professional, and I'm always available to my staff if they have any worries or concerns. If there was a genuine problem, the client would be reassigned, but that would be the exception rather than the rule. I can quite categorically say that Vivien never complained of any unwanted attention or obsessive behaviour from clients. Plus, of course, my unit specialises in dealing with young offenders, so there is the age difference."

"We will need a list of her clients."

"There are set procedures to follow." Jane reached for a file on her desk. "In anticipation of the request, I have printed them out for you."

Peter took the file. "Thank you for taking the time, but I'm sure our clerical staff have the matter in hand." Returning Jane's smile, he added, "How does your partner feel about your close relationships with male clients?"

Smoothly Jane replied, "My partner is fully supportive of my work and doesn't have any insecurity issues." Flashing a perfect smile, she added, "In there you will find details of Vivien's work schedule and a list of her clientele, which are already in the public domain. Also, the address of the client she visited on the afternoon of her death. I have spoken to the family already this morning. They understand they may have been the last people to have seen her alive and are happy to help the police in any way they can."

"That will probably be our next port of call," Peter said. "Could you tell us a little more about her last client of the day?"

Wheeling her chair to the other side of her desk, she said, "I'm afraid much of her file is confidential. How much they choose to share with you when you contact them is entirely up to them." She dropped eye contact and pulled a fresh file from the neat pile on the side of her desk. She looked up and said, "Do let me know if we can help you further."

Covering his irritation at their abrupt dismissal, Peter rose and said, "Thank you for your time. I trust you have no objection to us speaking to Vivien's co-workers who are in the office today."

With her head buried in the file, Jane gave a wave of her hand. "You may, but I expect you to respect that if they have appointments booked, they take priority."

"Of course," Peter replied. "And could you tell us where you were Wednesday evening?"

Jane gave Peter a withering look before silently walking into the small side room. She reappeared moments later carrying a handbag which she plonked onto the desk in front of Peter. After a quick search, she handed over a restaurant receipt and a theatre ticket stub. "I had a meal with my partner at the Goldbrick House on Park Street and then watched Sweeny Todd at Birstall Hippodrome." She held out her hand for the receipts to be returned. "Satisfied?"

"Very," Peter replied.

"What did you think of Pirelli?" Fiona asked.

"A talented singer but during the performance, there was obviously something wrong with his voice," Jane replied.

SIX

Vivien's co-workers all corroborated what they already knew. She was well-liked, generous and kind but a little naïve and too trusting at times. They were aware there was an injunction against her husband who they knew vaguely through work functions and mostly disliked.

Before they left, Jane Salt came out of her office and handed Peter a sheet of paper. "I've spoken to my superior and have jotted down a few notes about the last client Vivien visited. A young woman by the name of Ellen Bassett. She was the victim of a violent con man some years ago. The attack left her with severe physical injuries and deep psychological scars. I understand she remains terrified of the company of men and generally plays mute in their presence." With a bright smile, she concluded, "I hope that won't cause you too many difficulties."

Handing the sheet to Fiona without reading it, Peter replied, "I'm sure we'll manage."

Walking along the corridor, Peter said to Fiona, "If it is that big a deal, you can interview her, while I'll speak to the parents. I doubt the family will be able to add much to our investigations unless they saw something after she left. Their house isn't that far from where her body was found so the obvious assumption has to be she met her attacker shortly after leaving them, so we might get lucky." Tapping the control panel next to the lift doors he added, "Has the dog walker, Kathy something-or-other got back to you yet."

"No, I'll keep trying."

In the lift, Fiona pulled out the single sheet of paper covered in neat handwriting. She looked up when the lift door opened on the ground floor. "Well, how's that for a coincidence? Ellen Bassett is the young girl knocked from her bicycle by that Creer guy mentioned on the radio earlier. Plus, wait for this, she was pregnant with his baby at the time. At least we know exactly where he was when Vivien was attacked, so totally irrelevant but a strange coincidence all the same."

Peter stopped in his tracks. "Unless Rob Creer was the prison inmate Vivien's husband got his knickers in a twist about." He shook his head and carried on walking. "It's probably just one of those things, but I am going to check whether Vivien did have any contact with this Creer character. There could be something in it."

"Stranger things have happened."

"I wonder what the girl is doing down here. I understood the accident happened in the Midlands not far from where Creer lived."

◆ ◆ ◆

The Bassetts' home, Park Farm, was a rambling ivy-covered, Cotswold stone farmhouse with a range of outbuildings in the popular picturesque village of Topworth. They were halfway along the garden path when the front door was opened by a slight lady in a swirling long skirt. There were dark lines under her eyes, and her cheekbones were pronounced. Her piercing blue eyes darted over them before she poked her head out the door and looked past them, checking along the lane, satisfied there was no one in sight. Gripping the door tightly she said in a husky voice, "Come in. Come in. I'm Lucy Bassett, Ellen's mother."

In the corridor, they passed an attractive brunette looking immaculate in moleskin trousers and a simple but expensively cut pale blue button-down shirt. Her classy look was topped off with a silk scarf jauntily knotted at her neck. Although she appeared to be a similar age to Lucy Bassett, there was a youthful glow to her skin, and her upright athletic posture suggested she took great care of her health. She greeted them with a hello and a broad smile, showing a set of dazzling white teeth likely to make the best Hollywood stars envious. "Ciao Lucy. I'll pop in and say hi to Ellen on my way out," she said, kissing Lucy on the cheek. "You know where I am if you need me for anything. You only have to call."

"Thank you, Kathy, for everything. Some days I wonder what I'd do without you. If you could remind Ellen the police will be over to see her shortly that would be brilliant," Lucy said.

"Of course. I'll reassure her as much as I can." Kathy gave Peter and Fiona another smile. "I'll leave you all to it. Nice to meet you both," she added before continuing towards the front door.

Lucy directed them into a pleasant lounge before nervously flitting between that room and the kitchen offering them a range of drinks and snacks. When she finally settled into a rocking chair, she immediately lit a cigarette before offering the packet around. "Sorry I should have asked. Would you like one?"

Balancing a cup of tea and an assortment of cakes on her lap, Fiona declined for both of them, "Neither of us smoke." While Peter savoured a homemade walnut cake,

Fiona said, "We understood Ellen lived here with you?"

Drawing hard on her cigarette, Lucy held the smoke in her lungs before replying, in her throaty, raspy voice, "Ellen lives a semi-independent life next door." She released the smoke before repeatedly stubbing out the cigarette in an overflowing ashtray. "We converted an empty barn over the old stable block for her. Things were becoming very strained between us living under the same roof. Despite her problems, she has the same desires as other young women." She drummed her fingers on the arm of the rocking chair. "You do understand Ellen may not be able to help you very much? Since the accident... Well, she isn't the same and doesn't always understand what is going on."

A tall, gaunt man with a couple of days' dark stubble on his face, wearing farm overalls joined them. His dark, hooded eyes looked straight through them as if they were ghosts only existing in his peripheral vision. "She's left then?"

Before lighting up another cigarette, Lucy announced, "This is my husband, Ian."

Peter discarded his cup and saucer on the floor next to his feet and rose to greet him. "Mr Bassett, we're here to see your daughter, Ellen."

Ignoring Peter's outstretched hand, Ian selected a framed photograph of a happy smiling girl in a pale blue satin ball gown from the mantelpiece.

Through a cloud of smoke, Lucy said, "Ian?" as he stood frozen, staring down at the picture in his hand, reliving a moment from another time.

Withdrawing from wherever his mind had visited, Ian crossed the room and thrust the photograph into Fiona's hands. "My Ellen was once like you. Intelligent and beautiful with the world at her feet. She could have been anything she wanted to be." Anger flickered across his face. "Bloody media portrayed her as a Lolita. You lot weren't much better. And now I hear on the radio he's receiving top medical care, after sustaining a minor scratch no doubt. Shame whoever attacked him didn't do a good enough job. If I got my hands on him..." Ian's chest heaved under the strain of containing his inner anguish.

"She was a victim like the others. Probably his greatest victim. He took her life as surely as..."

"Mr Bassett," Peter interrupted. "We're here to ask about Vivien Morse, your daughter's social worker. We believe Ellen may have been the last person to have seen her alive prior to her attack."

Ian's fists tightened while he continued to stand over Fiona, oblivious to Peter's words.

Fiona met his unwavering stare. "What happened to your daughter, Mr Bassett?"

"Rob Creer. The evil bastard Rob Creer is what happened to my daughter. Have you heard of him?"

Looking down at the photograph and back up at Ian, Fiona

slowly said, "I think so. Was he responsible for a string of cons and burglaries up north a few years back? If I remember rightly, something went very wrong during his final burglary, and he killed someone."

Ian nodded encouragingly. "Yes, the bastard. He had the gall to claim at his trial that he had no recollection of the murder. He was so good at fooling people I worried his doctors may have convinced the jury it was true. Did you know he was an elected conservative councillor for the town of Brierly? Oh yes, he moved in all the right circles. Conning people into thinking he was an honest businessman. He used his contacts to find out when people were away from their homes and businesses before robbing them blind."

Ian paced across the room. "He is still in prison paying for those crimes, though. Wasting taxpayers' money and now charming young nurses. He should be rotting in hell for all he's done."

"How did your daughter become involved with him?"

Bitterness contorted Ian's features as he continued, "He took advantage of her youth and inexperience. Tricked her into believing he was in love with her and needed her to survive. She wasn't the only woman he tricked, but she was so young and innocent. It must have been like taking candy from a baby. That's all she was. My little baby. She was prepared to sacrifice everything for that monster but when the noose tightened around him, he...he..."

"Why don't you sit down, love, and I'll go and make a fresh pot of tea," Lucy suggested.

Ian raised his head and stared at the ceiling, his knuckles white over his clenched fists. "When they closed in on him, despite all the innocent love she offered him, he turned on her. She didn't know about the violent details of his crimes. She was begging him to give himself up and get help. She was prepared to wait for him. But that evil shit led her on. He had no intention of giving himself up. She was cycling out to meet him that day, believing they were going to visit the police station together voluntarily. The swine drove his fancy Porsche directly at her and left her for dead in the road. Left her as though she was nothing more than a stray dog."

"I'm truly sorry about what happened to Ellen. I appreciate how difficult it must be for you, but today we really need to talk about Ellen's social worker," Fiona said. "We want to find out whether she said anything to Ellen on her last visit. Something which may give us a clue as to what happened to her after she left here. Maybe even a name of who she might have been going to meet?"

Ian took the picture from Fiona and reverently placed it back onto the mantelpiece. "Yet another young woman you've failed to protect." He marched across the room, slamming the door shut behind him as he left. The pounding of his heavy footsteps was followed by the front door opening and closing and a car engine starting up. The silence in the lounge was pierced by the sound of Lucy inhaling and exhaling smoke from her cigarette.

"Would you like to see Ellen now?" Lucy asked brightly, as though the previous ten minutes hadn't happened. Before they reached the front door, she said, "Please try not to upset her. She knows what has happened to Vivien, but she gets confused very easily, and it is difficult to calm her down once something has set her off. There is one other thing I should tell you. She pretends a rag doll she calls, 'My Future,' is her baby."

Turning to close the door behind the three of them, Lucy continued as they crossed the yard area, "When she was unconscious in the hospital it was discovered she was nearly four months pregnant with his baby. She carried it full term, but as you'll see, she was obviously in no fit state of mind to care for the little tyke. The child would have always been a reminder, so we thought it for the best to put him up for adoption. We play along with her little game. I just thought I should pre-warn you both."

SEVEN

To avoid the water-filled potholes they zigzagged across the yard that separated the farmhouse from a range of old stone outbuildings. At the base, Lucy invited them to climb a flight of stone steps ahead of her to the second level. Despite the cutting cold wind, she halted once she reached the top. She looked back over the farmhouse and into the far distance while gripping the metal railing. "I'll just finish my cigarette here. Ellen doesn't like me smoking around the baby." Inhaling deeply on her cigarette and keeping her face turned away from them, her hair was blown in all directions. "I'm sure you think we're nuts, but it's easier not to trouble her in the first place than to deal with the aftermath."

"I'm sure you act in your daughter's best interests," Fiona said, glaring at Peter who was rolling his eyes while stamping his feet to keep warm.

Lucy shrugged, oblivious to the looks Fiona and Peter exchanged behind her. "Back in the day, the grooms would have lived here. The old stables are still there beneath us. We use them for storage now. We thought it would be helpful for Ellen to have some independence. Setting her up here seemed the ideal solution. She has her own space, but we are on hand at all times."

"When did you move down here from Birmingham?" Peter asked.

"Shortly after Ellen's accident. I couldn't stand living there a moment longer. I was slowly losing my mind. If it wasn't bad enough every day passing the spot that monster ploughed into our daughter and ignoring the hushed whispers of neighbours, we continued to be hounded by the press and odd strangers who came to gawp at us. We were under siege and constantly forced to defend ourselves from a never-ending onslaught of curiosity and accusations. I was suffocating under the unwanted attention, and petrified Ian might snap and attack one of them."

"Is your husband a violent man?" Peter asked.

Lucy shook her head vehemently. "Under normal circumstances not at all. But we were under a great deal of stress at the time, and they were all so intrusive. They had long-lens cameras, went through our dustbins and tried to gain access to our home at every opportunity. We just wanted to be left alone. Out here, away from prying eyes, seemed the perfect hideaway. I even believed for a short while I could heal and rebuild my broken family."

"It's certainly very isolated out here. Did Vivien Morse always visit Ellen alone in her own flat?" Peter asked.

"Sometimes if it was pleasant weather, they went for a walk or Ellen would show her the animals, especially if there were new arrivals."

"Do you know if they went for a walk on her last visit?"

Lucy shook her head. "It was a grey and dreary day." Balancing herself on the metal rail, she lifted her left leg and stubbed out her cigarette on the heel of her boot before slipping the butt end into her pocket. "It wouldn't do to leave my cigarette ends out here," she said apologetically.

Peter looked across to the large patio windows at the rear of the main house. "Did you see Vivien leave your property the last time she visited?"

"Yes. She gave me a little wave as she reversed out." Lucy stepped up to the front door and knocked loudly. "Ellen darling, it's mummy. The nice policeman I told you about earlier is here." Turning her attention to Peter, she said, defensively, "We don't spy on our daughter, but we do keep a close eye on her for her own good."

"I understand," Peter replied, glancing across the courtyard. With the main house behind and both sides enclosed by eight-foot-high stone walls, the area was a secure compound. The only exit was via the gate next to the main house. "Do you know if Ellen stayed in for the rest of the day after Vivien left?"

"Yes. I'm positive she did. She doesn't leave the farm by herself, but she does sometimes go out to the fields to see her old pony. Being such a dull day, it was already getting dark when Vivien left. So, when I popped over to check on Ellen, I turned on the security lights. If Ellen left her flat later, I would have been alerted straight away by the floodlights coming on."

The front door opened, expelling a blast of hot air.

Kathy, the women they'd passed earlier in the main house, held the door and ushered them in. "Come in. We don't want to let in the cold. I'm just leaving." Looking directly at Peter, she added, "I understand you may wish to speak to me later." She held out her hand. "I'm Kathy, Kathy Hooper. I found that poor woman out in the woods."

"We've been trying to get hold of you. We understood you were at work," Fiona said.

"I know, sorry. A lot of people are off sick at the moment plus I took some time off recently to organise a charity event. I've been working double shifts to try to make it up. I felt obliged to show up for work this morning despite the shock, but once I explained why I arrived late, I was sent home again."

"I should think so too. You turned quite pale earlier when I told you the poor woman was Ellen's social worker," Lucy said. "For a second I thought you were going to faint."

Kathy lowered her gaze to the floor as if ashamed of her moment of weakness. She looked up and gave Lucy a weak smile before saying to Peter, "I'm not sure how much I'll be able to help you, but you're welcome to come around after you've spoken to Ellen." Her air of confidence returned, and with a suggestive smile she added, "Or I will be at home later this evening if that would be a more convenient time."

"Any chance you could wait here?" Peter replied.

"Yes, of course. I'll wait in the main house for you."

After Kathy left, they realised Ellen had been behind her listening to their conversation. She stood with her legs apart, a few paces inside the narrow corridor with a vacant look on her face. Although slight, she blocked any further progress into the flat. Despite the thick woollen tights, she wore under a tiny miniskirt, her legs appeared long and shapely. It was hard to see her top half behind the bundle of blankets she clutched tight to her chest. With her head bowed over her precious bundle, long black hair fell forwards, hiding most of her face from view. She pointed at Peter. "I don't want him in here."

Peter stepped forward to speak, but Lucy placed a restraining hand on his elbow. Her grip was surprisingly strong while she said softly, "I'll take him outside, darling. Are you happy to talk to the female officer?"

Ellen gave a curt nod. Peter started to object before being cut off by Fiona, "I'm happy to stay and chat with Ellen while you speak to Kathy." She gave Ellen an encouraging smile, although it was unseen as Ellen's hair still covered her face.

As soon as Peter retreated with Lucy and Kathy, Ellen led Fiona through a small living room and into a dining area which was little more than an alcove. Windowless, the darkness was alleviated by a huge yellow sun with rays reaching the ceiling painted onto the far white wall. A multi-coloured rug covered most of the stone floor. A collection of mismatched wooden chairs around an orange table had been hand painted and varnished in bright primary colours. Fiona lowered herself onto a green chair while Ellen selected a red one on the opposite side of the table.

"Did you design and paint this room?" Fiona asked. "It's very cheery."

"Thank you. I think it is important to provide a colourful, stimulating environment for my daughter," Ellen replied, holding her bundle close to her chest. She glanced up briefly, giving Fiona a shy smile before hiding her face again.

"The lady who just left seemed very nice."

"Aunt Kathy. She's been very good to us. She likes to check in on

Little Future. She buys her dresses and toys all the time. I do get worried, though, when she asks to hold her. That's not allowed until she's a little older. Without a father figure around, it is very important she has a strong bond with me as her mother."

Fiona pulled her notepad and pen from her pocket and tentatively said, "I understand your mother has told you Vivien Morse was attacked some time yesterday evening, after visiting you earlier in the day." Seeing no reaction, Fiona continued, "I'm trying to find out what happened to her after she left you. I was hoping you might be able to help me."

Ellen rocked her bundle in time with an inaudible rhythm. "I don't know what happened to her. Why do you think I should?" The silent rhythm increased in tempo. "Do you think I done her in? That's impossible. I never leave here. I wouldn't harm anyone. Make love, not war. That's my motto."

"No, no, not at all," Fiona was quick to reassure Ellen. "I was hoping maybe Vivien told you where she was going before she left. Don't worry if she didn't. Even an indication as to her mood that afternoon would be useful."

"You don't think I took her to the woods and bashed her head in with a rock, do you?"

Taken aback, Fiona replied, "Is there any reason why you would want to do that?" Smiling at Ellen, she tried to recall what had been reported in the morning newspapers.

Ellen cocked her head to one side mouthing Fiona's words to herself as she considered the question. "Nah, she was nice and helped me with the baby. That's why she visited. She was always very concerned about the little 'un's well-being. She knew lots of stuff about how to care for a baby and give them the best possible start in life, but I didn't like it when she tried to take my Future from me."

"Take her from you?"

"Yes. She said it was time she was fully examined. Developmental checks or something. I said no way. I can tell everything is fine. I would know if anything was wrong. Mummy always knows best. Do you have a baby?"

"No, not at the moment."

"Shame. If you did, then you would understand the bond between mother and child. In the end, Vivien agreed there was no need for her to try to take my baby from me for some daft tests."

Scribbling on her notepad, Fiona asked, "Did she ever suggest anything like that before?"

Ellen shook her head. "No never. She'd always been very kind and respectful."

"Do you think she was being kind during her last visit?"

"Not when she was trying to touch my Future."

"How did that make you feel?"

"Angry. But then she said it didn't matter. We could do it another day, so it was okay."

Fiona asked, "Why do you think she was bashed by a rock in the woods?"

Ellen studied Fiona for a while from under her long fringe. "She was, wasn't she? That's what mummy said. She'd been bashed in the woods, and that was why you wanted to see me. What are you writing down? The doctor writes things when he talks to me. I don't like it."

Putting her notes to one side, Fiona said, "Did you talk about other things with Vivien?"

"He wants to have sex with me?"

"Who does?" Fiona asked.

"The doctor."

"Did you mention that to Vivien?"

Ellen paused briefly before replying, "No. Occasionally we'd talk about boyfriends and all, but mostly it was baby stuff."

"Did Vivien have a boyfriend?"

"Yes." Ellen put her fingers to her lips, "Shush. It was a secret. He wrote to her a lot." Ellen looked up triumphantly. "I was the only person she talked to about him. She couldn't trust no one else, you see. Only me and Future."

Itching to pick up her pen again, Fiona asked, "What was his name?"

Ellen dropped her chin onto her chest and started to hum to

herself. She raised her head abruptly and said, "He didn't have no name. Not that I remember anyways. I do know he wasn't going to be hush-hush for much longer. They were going to be together very soon, but they had to do something first. I don't know what it was. Just that it was going to happen soon."

"Divorce proceedings, maybe?" Fiona suggested, craning her neck to see Ellen's face.

Ellen continued to keep her head down as she rocked her bundle of blankets. "Maybe. I don't understand people who divorce. If you love someone, then that's forever. You don't stop loving them and get a divorce. That doesn't make any sense. Does that make sense to you?"

Ignoring the question, Fiona said, "Earlier you claimed you never leave here. Surely you go out sometimes. Your mother said you showed Vivien the baby animals."

Ellen looked directly at Fiona for the first time. "I'll only leave the farm boundaries when my love returns. He won't be bothered by my disfigured face." She pulled her hair away from her face before adding, "Would you want people staring at you if you were scarred like this?"

Fiona looked into Ellen's pale blue eyes before studying a blemish-free complexion, snub nose and rosebud lips. "But you're beautiful!"

Ellen pulled back her black fringe. "Look closer," she ordered, pushing her face up close to Fiona. "Ugly. Ugly. Ugly."

Despite a close inspection, the only minor defect Fiona could see was a slight indentation below her hairline. Smelling mints on the girl's breath and feeling uncomfortable with the invasion of her personal space, Fiona sat back, unsure how to respond. "When do you think your love will return?"

"Very soon. He'll scoop me up and carry us both away on a prancing stallion." Ellen stood and rocked her baby while singing softly, "Hush now baby, please don't cry. Daddy's going to buy you a Mockingbird."

Not quite believing she was joining in the charade, Fiona asked, "Have you kept in contact with your baby's father?"

Ellen shook her head violently. "They took him away. I'm not allowed to see him. They want to take my Future away, but I won't let them." She hugged the doll deep within the bundle of blankets tight to her chest. "No one is going to take my little Future away."

"Do you ever write to him?"

Ellen started to nod, her body rocking backwards and forwards. "They took him to a bad place. No one can contact him there. The place is run by aliens."

Fiona waited as Ellen started to hum the earlier lullaby. Once the song finished, she asked, "What's his name?" Ellen ceased rocking and put her finger to her lips. "Shush, the walls have ears." She leaned in close to Fiona and whispered, "Robbie," before resuming her singing. "And if that Mockingbird…"

Fiona slipped her notebook into her bag and swung it over her shoulder as she stood to leave. "Thank you for your time, Ellen. I'll see myself out."

"Yes, that might be best. Our little Future needs my full attention now. Daddy will be angry if he discovers I didn't care for her properly," Ellen said, before returning to her singing.

Fiona left the overheated flat with a sense of unease. Despite it sending a shiver down her spine, the cold air outside was a welcome relief from the oppressive sense of sadness she'd felt inside. She spotted Peter waiting in the car in the courtyard. She hurried down the steps, reaching the car door as huge raindrops started to fall and bounce off the myriad of puddles surrounding the car.

"How did you get on?" Peter asked, hardly giving her a chance to close the passenger door before driving off.

"She creeped me out a little, and she wasn't able to add much except she claims Vivien had a boyfriend."

"Interesting nobody else has mentioned one. We're heading over to Vivien's house now and collecting the door key from her neighbour. Maybe she knows something more about this unknown boyfriend. What was your overall impression of Ellen?"

"A severely damaged mind. I'm not sure her living there alone with her pretend baby is the best form of treatment for her."

"As we're not psychiatrists, that's not really our concern. Did she seem violent to you?" Peter asked.

"In certain circumstances, I think her capable of attacking Vivien, but I doubt she'd have the nounce to cover up her actions afterwards."

"But her parents would," Peter pointed out.

"It's a possibility. But then they would want to restrict our access to their daughter for fear of what she might say. Lucy had no worries about leaving me alone with her."

"Good point. Anything else?"

"She admitted Vivien annoyed her during the last visit by wanting to hold the 'baby.' She claimed she wanted to carry out some developmental tests and she only backed down when Ellen refused to hand her doll over."

"Bizarre."

"How did you get on with Kathy?"

With a smug smile, Peter replied, "I was asked out to dinner."

"Seriously? Are you going?"

"Yes seriously, but no I'm not. I'm a happily married man. Well, married anyway."

Grinning, Fiona asked, "Other than a dinner date, did you get anything else? According to Lucy, her reaction to discovering the identity of Vivien seemed stronger than actually finding her."

"I noticed that comment from Lucy as well. Kathy claimed to have never met Vivien and Lucy couldn't remember whether they'd bumped into each other at the farm or not. When Lucy left the room, I questioned Kathy about her reaction, and she admitted to a one-night stand with the husband, Nigel. She didn't have a horse to ride, so she followed the Opening Meet on foot and had too much of the Stirrup Cup."

"What's the Stirrup Cup?"

"Traditionally Port and brandy. It's what the huntsmen drink before setting off. She went on to The Old Bell Inn afterwards. Nigel had been in there a few times before and flirted with her. One thing led to another, and they became very drunk and spent the night together. She had expected to have to give him the brush-off, but she hasn't seen him since. She was very quick to give herself an alibi for Wednesday afternoon and evening."

"A good one?" Fiona asked.

"Pretty good. She was at work until three in the afternoon and spent the rest of the day and evening preparing and then attending a cocktail party to raise funds for an injured jockey. We could double-check it later if needs be. When Lucy returned, I asked whether either of them had noticed a man dressed in Druid robes in the area. Although they hadn't, Kathy seemed fascinated by the idea."

"Lucy looked more like the type to have a bit of an eccentric streak in her and be interested in that sort of thing," Fiona said. "Kathy seemed very pleasant, but also very conservative in her outlook."

"Looks can be deceptive," Peter replied. "She certainly wasn't backwards in inviting me out for dinner."

Vivien's home was a rented Victorian semi-detached house on the edge of Birstall. It fronted a busy main road that carried a constant stream of traffic into and out of Birstall city centre. The neighbour was polite, but said she'd only spoken a couple of times in passing to Vivien. She only held the spare key as she was employed as a cleaner by the letting agency that managed the house.

The two bedroomed house was exceptionally clean and tidy inside. Renovation work to update the house had been done in a way that combined the period features with modern facilities. Minimal furniture, one used plate and set of cutlery on the kitchen draining board and a singular toothbrush in the small bathroom confirmed Vivien as someone who lived alone. The cupboards and wardrobes indicated a smart but conservative dresser. There were no personal touches to reflect the occupier's personality anywhere. The spare bedroom was used as a study. Correspondence was neatly organised in files on the bottom shelf of an orderly bookcase.

After an hour of poking around and finding nothing of interest, they returned the key to the neighbour and headed back to the station. Fiona rejected Peter's suggestion of a quick stop in a pub, and they went their separate ways home from the car park.

EIGHT

Peter was preoccupied during the morning meeting led by Fiona. He mulled over the written reports e-mailed to him overnight, and only half listened to the verbal updates.

"Sir," Fiona nudged him in the ribs. "We're finished."

Peter took his place at the front of the room. "On the face of it, from what we've discovered so far Nigel Morse has accounted for his whereabouts, and nothing incriminating has been found at the house. Vivien's life assurance policy is minimal, covering only funeral costs, so her death isn't going to provide him with a windfall. However, she was planning to file for divorce, and that can get messy. We haven't got an exact time of death, he has a history of violence against women, and we only have his word about the stop at the motorway services. It would be tight but just about possible that if he made good time driving back from his appointments, he could have met his wife after she left Ellen Bassett at Park Farm."

"Are there any receipts from the service station?" Ward asked.

Humphries half stood. "Apparently not. He claims to have bought a coffee with cash and didn't keep a receipt," he said, before allowing his bulk to fall back into his chair.

"Humphries has checked, and this is pretty standard practice for him," Peter continued from the front of the room. "He only claims back full meals on his expenses. But he is very vague about this time period at the service station, so I'm not completely discounting him just yet. I want you to continue digging.

Talk to his neighbours, work colleagues and friends. Anyone he's been in contact with since he moved down here. A quick check with his previous employers in the Midlands wouldn't go amiss either. I'm planning on paying him a visit later today, so if anything is discovered, I'd like the details as quickly as possible. I want to see how he reacts to a bit of pressure."

"Sweating like a pig, mostly," Humphries said. "He has a serious personal hygiene problem."

Ignoring Humphries' aside, Peter continued, "So far all of Vivien's friends and contacts have confirmed she was a generous, friendly person with no enemies. There appears to be consensus she was going to be far happier without her husband around, but I can't see any mention in the statements of a new boyfriend. According to Ellen Bassett, she had a secret boyfriend. Go back and find out his name."

"Yes, sir," Smith replied.

"According to the initial report, although Vivien's clothes were interfered with, she was not sexually assaulted. It is possible we're looking for a jealous woman, so when you discover who her secret boyfriend was, go and check out his wife." Registering the look on the officer's face, Peter said, "Yes, Humphries? What is it?"

"Nothing really sir," Humphries replied, half rising from his chair again. "It's just that I don't think there was anyone special in Vivien's life."

"Sit down, Humphries. We'll talk about that in a minute." Peter turned the laptop screen he'd been examining to face DS Abbie Ward and DC Litten. "This is a complete list of all of Vivien's recent client visits."

Abbie stepped forwards to examine the screen. After she'd looked, Peter turned the computer around to face him. "I want you two to prioritise anyone with a record of violence and put them at the top of the list to interview. Anyone who might have had cause to hold a grudge against Vivien Morse is of interest."

Closing the laptop, Peter continued, "We'll be taking a closer look at the Bassett family, as the last known people to see Vivien alive, especially the father, Ian Bassett. There's a lot of anger there and ..."

"Is oddness the word you're looking for?" Fiona suggested.

"Yes, quite. There is something not right about the family. Amongst other things, Fiona and I will be looking into their background. Also," Peter raised his hand to get everyone's attention as they were starting to fidget, preparing to leave. "This may be a complete red herring, but both families, Bassett and Morse, originate from the same area of Birmingham. If any of you discover there are any other connections or instances where their paths crossed previously, either up there or since moving to our area, contact one of us immediately."

"Sir?" Humphries said. "I don't know if this is relevant, but Vivien's house was broken into about ten days ago. She was really upset because, although nothing was taken, the intruder clearly went through her personal correspondence."

"Do you know if it was reported?"

"I don't know. She told me about it because she wanted to confide in someone more than anything. Talk about how violated she felt."

Peter glared at Smith, who was pulling faces and hugging himself as if in an embrace. "Thank you, Humphries. That's helpful. It could be nothing or it could suggest Vivien either had or knew something somebody else was interested in." Peter stroked his chin before adding, "Check whether any of her friends or work colleagues have had break-ins in the last few months."

"How is Nigel Morse connected to Rob Creer, sir?" Abbie Ward asked, looking quizzically at the whiteboard.

"I'm not sure he is at this stage. I was playing about with ideas and added Creer's name because of his connection to Ellen Bassett. We know Vivien visited prison inmates under some visitor charity scheme right up to when they moved from the Birmingham area. We're still awaiting confirmation of which inmates Vivien visited and whether the list does include Creer. Although he denies it, I suspect these prison visits were a deciding factor in Nigel insisting they change location. He claims he doesn't know the names of the individual prisoners, but I think he's lying. Keep me updated throughout the day."

Over the sound of chattering, he added, "I almost forgot. I received a complaint recently about a newcomer to the area who dresses as a Druid priest. Has anyone seen him?" Peter looked out at a sea of blank faces.

"He is new to the area and has been spotted acting suspiciously around Lower Woods and allegedly has looked through people's windows. Those woods are a good six or seven miles from where Vivien was found, but it is something to keep in mind if you come across him. Okay, so what are you waiting for? Get going. Except you, Humphries. I want a quick word in my office."

As he passed Fiona, he said, "While we have our chat could you contact Shoreham Prison to check if Vivian did visit Rob Creer on a regular basis, or any other inmates held there, especially any who have been released recently. Her parents are travelling down today and have asked to speak with us. They'll be here in about an hour."

Abbie caught Fiona's attention as she picked up the phone to ring the prison. "Tonight, at my place? Around eight o'clock?"

Fiona gave her the thumbs up before dialling the number. During the call she watched Humphries re-join his colleagues after his private chat with Peter. There was jostling, laughing and joking before they set off to complete their duties. A wave of sadness hit her. She wasn't sure whether it was because she felt an outsider or whether she was missing Nick Tattner.

In theory, they all accepted the dangers of the job, but the loss of the young officer still upset her. She'd been getting along well with him, and he was due to be made up to a Detective Inspector when he was killed. Guilt flooded her mind when she recalled the tinge of jealousy she'd felt when Peter had taken him instead of her that evening, so she could attend her drama club meeting. But if he hadn't gone in her place, she might have been the one caught up in the explosion. A shiver ran down her spine at the thought.

Completing her call, she pushed open their office door. Deep in thought, Peter sat on the window ledge with his back towards the car park and Tibberton High Street below. "Everything go okay with Humphries?"

"He's staying on the case for now, but if you notice anything off about things, let me know," Peter said.

"Will do. He does seem a little blinkered at the idea she might have met someone else."

Pushing himself from the ledge, Peter asked, "How did you get on? Have any of the inmates Vivien Morse visited been released recently?"

"Not terribly well, I'm afraid. They've had computer problems in the past. They have a new system now, but apparently, some records have not been transferred over. They were able to confirm Vivien was a regular visitor, but it might take them a while to locate and go through the old records before they can confirm which inmates she visited. They're going to get back to me later today."

"Did you ask about Creer?"

"Yes. They couldn't tell me much other than the injuries he sustained weren't life-threatening. They hope he'll be on his way back to the prison soon."

"Meanwhile in other news," Peter joked. "Miss Lisle has confirmed our wandering Druid crept through her garden and right up to her living room window to take a look inside. I suggest before we re-interview Nigel Morse today, we go and find this Druid, even if it's only to discount him and stop local gossip."

"The timing of his arrival and his strange behaviour lurking about in the woods does suggest he could have been the attacker. He's a peeping tom if nothing else."

Drumming his fingers on the window sill, Peter said, "I'm not disagreeing with you. We do need to find this fellow as quickly as possible and question him, but I'm not going to base my judgement on the word of that busybody Glenys Pitman. If we arrested everyone she took a dislike to, there would be a lot of empty homes in the area. He could be a completely harmless person walking his dog. I know Mandy Lisle from the community watch meetings, and she is a little on the over-dramatic and hysterical side of normal. There's also the possibility he's seen something. A stranger often has a different perspective and notices things that locals no longer see."

When Peter continued to stare at the whiteboard, giving no indication he was going to move any time soon, Fiona said, "What's bothering you?"

"I can't tell you why or where Creer might fit in, but I have a strong gut feeling about a connection between him and the murder that's really annoying me. At first, I just thought it was a strange coincidence hearing his name on the radio like we did and then discovering his connection to Vivien's last client visit." Peter tapped the side of his head. "Problem is I can't get the idea out of my head that there is a connection we're not seeing."

Fiona pulled a wheeled office chair out from under the desk and sat to the side of him. "Maybe it's not a direct connection. I'm thinking out loud here, but how about Ian Bassett discovered Vivien used to regularly visit Creer in prison and was sympathetic towards the guy. He followed her from the farm and forced her to pull over in her car and walk into the woods. She tried to explain Creer was not all bad, and he completely lost it and battered her to death?"

"That gives Bassett motive and opportunity. We need to check his whereabouts and bring him in for questioning if needs be." Peter thought for a while before saying, "Or how about the boyfriend Vivien mentioned to Ellen is Creer? Nigel Morse discovered his wife hadn't broken off contact with Creer when they moved down here, and he didn't stop at the service station like he claims. He could have arranged to meet up with her after she left Ellen. They argued, and he could have battered her with a stick in a loss of temper before returning home and creating his celebratory alibi."

"Although technically he would have had time, it would take a pretty cool customer to wander down the local and act normally after beating his wife to death," Fiona said. "And that's assuming Vivien would have been prepared to meet with him in such an

57

isolated spot. I think it unlikely a normal person with their history of violence would agree to the meeting place."

"Define normal."

Fiona pulled a face. "Call it woman's intuition, but I just don't see it. Their recent contact has all been via solicitors. Why the sudden face-to-face meeting in such an odd location? I can imagine Nigel Morse as a schoolyard bully and a bit of a creep, thinking it is okay to push his wife around at home when he doesn't get his own way. He makes me think of a slimy slug likely to slither and lurk in dark corners being offensive when drunk. I can even imagine him stalking her and watching what she did at night. But I can't see Vivien happy to walk into the woods alone with him on a dark evening. Has anything been found in his car or house?"

Peter shook his head. "They haven't finished processing everything yet. If it was him, he wouldn't have had time to destroy every minute shred of evidence and create his alibi by spending the evening in the pub. So, we'll have to wait on their final report. Until then he remains our main suspect."

"If we go with the idea Vivien carried on a romance via correspondence with Creer, how do you think Ellen would have reacted if she found out? According to Ellen, they did talk about a boyfriend. She's crazy enough, and I could see her acting out of passion and rage," Fiona said.

"Interesting idea but I find it hard to believe Vivien could be that stupid. She must have been aware Creer was the person responsible for her client's condition. Even if she was exchanging love letters with him why on earth would she tell Ellen?" Peter slammed his palms on the desk. "Pull the Rob Creer file and have a look at the references to Ellen. Her father seemed to suggest the police regarded her as a willing partner rather than a victim. See if there's anything there to support their opinion. I'm going to contact the media to request another appeal for witnesses who might have seen Vivien after she left Park Farm. Once we've spoken to the parents, we'll pay Ian Bassett another visit."

❖ ❖ ❖

Vivien's parents arrived on time and carried the visible stain of a sudden bereavement into the room. Her father, a large man with a receding hairline, gripped his wife's hand tightly as though if he let go, he might lose her as well. While her father, Mr Waring, looked like he carried the weight of the world on his shoulders, his wife looked brittle and vulnerable as though grief had sucked all the vitality from her body.

"Please take a seat," Peter said, trying not to allow their misery to seep into his mind. "I'm very sorry for your loss, and we're doing all we can to find the person responsible."

Continuing to clasp his wife's hand, Mr Waring said, "Do you have a daughter?"

"Yes, yes I do."

"Then you know nothing you can say or do will change things for us. Our little girl is gone, and no one can bring her back. But to know her murderer will be punished for what he did will help a little. To see him walk away scott free would add to our unbearable pain."

"Do you have Nigel in custody?" Mrs Waring asked in a shaky voice. "You have no idea how it has been for us watching our once bubbly and confident daughter become increasingly withdrawn and doubtful. We thought once she left that animal she would be safe. Then this."

"Nigel Morse has been questioned as part of our investigations," Peter said carefully. "Could I ask when you first noticed there was a problem with your daughter's marriage?"

"As soon as the honeymoon was over. Initially, Viv was too proud to admit there was a problem and ask for help. When she couldn't hide her injuries, she refused to listen to reason and insisted he could change. But of course, a leopard never changes his spots. Talking as a mother to a father, please lock that terrible man away and save another family from what we're going through."

"If we find Nigel Morse is responsible for your daughter's death, I will do my utmost to bring him to trial, but at this stage, I can't make any promises."

Mr Waring stood, "Your promise to do your best is all we ask for. We wanted to see what type of man was dealing with our baby girl's case." He shook Peter's hand. "Thank you for seeing us. We won't take up any more of your time. We want you out there investigating the truth."

Mrs Waring said, "He really is a very cruel man. I'm only relieved they didn't have children. He made Vivien leave her dear little dog behind when she left. When you put him away, we want to adopt him in her memory."

"Just one last question. Do you know why your daughter finally left him? Was there a particularly nasty attack?" Peter asked.

"Not especially. It was more of a realisation he wasn't even apologising anymore for his violence and that he was never going to change."

Returning to his office after seeing the Warings out, Peter said, "Nice ordinary couple and from the witnesses we've spoken to, they brought up a loving and generous daughter. I've read all the psychology and know you attended the domestic violence course in London, so I accept you're the expert. But I can't help thinking it is always the kind and compassionate people who stay with violent partners."

"It is a lot more complicated than that. If the circumstances are right, anyone can become trapped in an abusive relationship."

"Really? I couldn't imagine a strong person like you ever getting yourself into that situation. Surely you'd bail at the first sign of a problem?"

The phone rang before Fiona had the opportunity to reply. Realising Peter's call was going to take a while, she sat at her desk to re-read the newspaper article that referred to Ellen as a Lolita. Her eyes scanned the words as her mind stubbornly focused on the thin line between a loving and a controlling relationship.

Peter finished his call and announced, "Leave whatever you're doing. I think we should have an early lunch out at The Bear and

Ragged Staff Inn."

Fiona studied Peter's face before saying, "Are you going to tell me why? You've got that look on your face." Peter pulled a stupid face. "You mean other than the fact it is the mid-point between Park Farm and where Vivien was found? Or it could be the landlord rang the newspaper after reading the article they ran yesterday to say she stopped in for a drink late Wednesday afternoon? With another woman."

Shutting down her laptop and grabbing her coat, Fiona said, "Why on earth didn't they tell us before?"

"The guy literally just contacted them. He was reading the paper on his break when he saw the appeal. While we're there, we can also see if the locals confirm that Ellen was telling the truth about never leaving the farm."

As they were about to leave, Fiona snatched up her desk phone on its first ring. She listened for a while before saying, "Could you give me the crime reference? It may be nothing or very relevant." She tapped it into the computer before calling Peter over. "Vivien did report the break-in at her flat. The report confirms nothing was taken but whoever broke in wasn't very adept at covering their tracks. Although she wasn't in the habit of taking work files home, as nothing of value was taken it was assumed they were searching for something connected to her work. Nigel was interviewed about it, but he was attending a soft toy convention in Scotland at the time, so they concluded it couldn't have been him. One very strange thing. Afterwards, she noticed her flat was covered in dog hairs."

NINE

A weak wintery sun made a welcome appearance after weeks of dismal grey weather. Recently the only variant in the daily forecast had been steady rain, heavy rain or complete deluges of rain causing flash floods. Despite the brief respite, the runoff from the fields ensured the lanes continued to resemble fast flowing rivers. The one benefit of The Bear and Ragged Staff Inn being in the base of the valley was as they dropped lower, the high hedges gave the car protection from the blustery winds. This was little comfort to Peter as he waited for a fallen branch to float past them before turning into the car park.

There were only a handful of cars huddled around the Inn's entrance plus a colourfully painted old Bedford van.

"This retro stuff is all the rage now, according to Amelia," Peter commented, eyeing up the huge red and yellow flowers painted on the side of the van. "Although this van looks like it may very well have been around during the original wave of hippies and flower power." So taken with the artwork, which included a larger than life naked girl, he stepped out of the car into a huge puddle. "Dammit. God, I'm sick of all this rain. I'm bloody soaked right through."

Fiona checked before stepping over a puddle on the passenger side. She laughed at Peter shaking each leg in turn while continuing to swear in the vain hope he could shake out the water from his drenched trousers and shoes. "Well, that doesn't sound much like peace and love. I guess you don't remember it all from the first time around."

"Hey, less of the cheek, young lady. I was born in the early seventies when it was all commercialised with Coca-Cola trying to teach the world to sing." With a final shake, he squelched his way up the stone steps leading to the front door. Holding the heavy oak door open for her he said, "We'd best go into the bar rather than leave puddles in the lounge area."

The bar was dimly lit with low beams skimming the top of Fiona's head. They could hear chatter from the lounge area, but despite the cackle of the welcoming fire, the bar appeared deserted. Peter rang the hand bell on the counter, and a young barman in a shirt and tie poked his head around the corner. "I'll be with you in a minute, sir," he called politely before disappearing back to the lounge area. Fiona picked up a menu while Peter walked along the row of beer pumps.

"It's very pricey," Fiona said, reading the menu. "But it is all made fresh to order."

"The range of real ales is pretty impressive," Peter said. Moments later he was engulfed in a soft, scented bear hug. Struggling to turn around, he found himself face deep in the ample bosom of Gladys Jones. He tried to pull back, but the embrace tightened, pulling him deeper into the soft rolls of fat.

"I've told you before, Gladys," a male voice from behind the bar said, "please put my customer down."

"Oh Jake, you're so funny," Gladys said, slightly relaxing her iron-like grip on Peter but not totally letting him go. "These are darling old friends of mine. Whatever they're having you must add it to my bill."

With an audible sigh, Jake said, "And when will you be settling your bill? Your tab is getting quite high."

"My dear man," a voice boomed from somewhere behind Gladys. "I will be settling this charming woman's bill this very evening."

"As you wish," Jake said, rolling his eyes. "What can I get you two to drink?" He looked over at the menu in Fiona's hand and added, "I'm afraid the chef has been sent home due to the weather, so I can only offer you bar snacks."

Peter wriggled free from Gladys and put his hand in his pocket. "It's quite okay, I'll be getting these." He stopped open-mouthed when he turned to address the man offering to buy their drinks and realised why Fiona had been struck dumb. Standing beside her was a giant of a man, stooping almost double to avoid the beams. He had a long, flowing white beard, and he held a rough looking wooden staff in one hand and a champagne flute in the other. He wore open-toed sandals and long white robes tied in the middle by a hessian rope. At his naked toes sat a shaggy-haired Lurcher-type dog watching the activity with a look of far greater intelligence than its owner. "I take it the painted van outside is yours?"

"Oh yes! Isn't Bertha a wonderful creature of beauty?"

"Darlings!" Gladys exclaimed. "I'd like you all to meet my new friend, Dick."

"Nice to meet you, Dick," Jake said. "But what do you all want to drink?"

Before Jake could scurry back to the lounge as soon as he put the drinks on the bar, Peter said, "I was hoping to talk to Adrian. He called earlier to say he'd be here."

Jake said, "You must be Peter Hatherall. Adrian said you would be coming in and asked me to apologise on his behalf. His mother has just fallen. She only lives up the road. He should be back within the hour."

"Thanks, we'll wait for him."

Gladys and her new friend had turned their attention to Fiona, so Peter showed Jake a picture of Vivien Morse. "Have you ever seen this woman?"

After a quick glance. Jake replied, "Sure, she's the lady who was attacked in Silver Lady Woods."

Peter slipped the photograph back into his pocket. "I mean have you ever seen her in here or anywhere else before she was assaulted?"

Jake slowly shook his head. "Sorry mate, I can't help you there."

"Were you working in here on Wednesday, late afternoon or

early evening?"

"Yup. Sad little life I lead. I came in just before eight. I always seem to be working here, but I've never seen her before."

"That evening was there anyone else unusual in the here? A stranger, or someone acting suspiciously? Watching out a front window maybe?"

Jake rested his forearm over a beer pump and whispered in his ear, "Only that freak Gladys has just introduced as Dick."

Peter was unable to ask more as Gladys reappeared, linked arms with him and manhandled him towards a table in an alcove. "You must tell me everything you've been up to." With a nod of her head, she enthused, "Dick is dying to meet you."

Once they were seated, Dick stood and towered over them. "My canine friend desires a breath of fresh air. We will re-join this pleasant soiree thereafter." With a swish of his robes revealing dainty white ankles, Dick made his way towards the door. He turned when he was half-way across the room to give a little wave of a handkerchief. "Ta ta, my lovely."

"Isn't he to die for?" Gladys exclaimed, fanning her burning skin with a beer mat.

"Totally," Peter replied. "Where on earth did you meet him?"

Not registering the sarcastic tone, Gladys put her arm around Peter and pulled him towards her. She beckoned Fiona on the opposite side of the table to lean in closer. "Now my darlings, you mustn't go upsetting yourself if Dick is a little distant when he hears of your profession. I'm positive with a little effort by you any concerns can be overcome, and you will become firm friends. He really is a most delectable creature."

"Why should our profession concern him?" Peter asked gruffly. "Does he have something to hide?"

"No, silly." Gladys gave Peter a girlish light tap on the shoulder and giggled. "He is a wronged man," she said, shaking her head sadly. Her mood lifted as quickly as it had fallen. "You're just the man to help reinstate his impeccable reputation."

"Why would I need or even want to do that?" Peter asked.

"Justice, my precious. Justice. Now don't try to deny how jolly important that is to you." She wagged her finger in front of Peter's face. "There's no point trying to lie to little old me."

"Sorry," Fiona interrupted. "Where did you meet him? I think I must have missed that part."

Gladys let go of Peter and cupped Fiona's face in her hands. "Oh, my little cherub. You haven't changed, have you? Still so serious and intense. Relax. Lose those pesky inhibitions and embrace the wonders all about you." Gladys released her face and sat back with a smile. "We haven't long," she said, glancing towards the door looking mysterious. "I met him when visiting my dear brother, Bert."

Peter banged his glass on the table, narrowly avoiding spitting out a mouthful of Old Peculiar beer. "You met him in prison? Please tell me he was a fellow visitor and not an inmate."

"He was wrongly convicted by a cruel and inept system. He was released as soon as those buffoons realised their mistake. He was stoical and strong on the inside. A lesser being would be twisted and bitter after all he went through. But not my gentle Dick. He is quite philosophical about the whole dreadful experience. As a trusted and loyal friend, I would like to have his name cleared. In fact, I insist."

"Do be careful," Fiona warned. "How well do you really know him?"

"Well enough."

"Remind me again the name of the prison," Peter said, his eyes still wide in utter amazement.

"Shoreham."

Peter's voice went up an octave. "The high-security wing?"

"Yes, but I can tell from the look on your face that you are judging him with no knowledge of the ghastly miscarriage of justice. That is most ungentlemanly of you, and quite frankly I'm surprised and a little disappointed in you."

"Gladys?" Fiona interrupted. "Do you know if Dick met Rob Creer when he was in there?"

"Why don't you ask him yourself," Gladys replied, nodding towards the open door.

Peter took a gulp of his beer and stood. "I'm getting another drink. Same again for everyone?"

Dick slapped Peter on the back, causing him to stumble forwards a few steps. "Wonderful idea, my good man. I'll assist you in your endeavours. Leave these two charming ladies to chitter chatter and powder their parts."

Fiona gave a pained expression and silently mouthed to Peter, "Powder my parts?" Out loud she said, "Just water for me, please."

TEN

Waiting at the bar for their drinks to be served, Peter ignored the bewildered looks Dick received from two new customers sitting on bar stools. A quick glance told him Dick was oblivious to their attention. He concluded he was either so used to it that it no longer bothered him, or he really was totally away with the fairies in a world of his own. He racked his brain for a safe conversation that wouldn't cause alarm if overheard at the bar while a million possible questions flooded his mind. "Nice dog you have there. He's very well trained."

"She is young with much to learn." Dick's voice became taut and angry. "My previous dog was lost due to police corruption. She believed I'd abandoned her and died of a broken heart while I was incarcerated in a dreadful place. It is always the innocent who pay the highest price while those at fault escape unscathed." With a pious look to the ceiling, he added, "One should still be thankful for small mercies. Here I am, a man of freedom."

Peter ordered the drinks, sharing a look of bemusement with Jake. While the drinks were being served, he turned to Dick and said, "I'm sorry about your earlier dog, but this one is lovely. What's her name?" He bent forwards to pat the dog. He straightened up abruptly banging his head on a beam, when the dog growled and curled up its top lip showing a fine set of sharp white teeth.

Unconcerned by the aggressive reaction, Dick said, "Colin does not like her aura entered by those she has not invited."

The drinks appeared on the bar and Peter said to Dick,

"Why don't you take the drinks over to the ladies? I'll settle the bill."

Dick was happy with the arrangement and quickly turned to leave, his large hands easily carrying the four drinks without any need for a tray. Pocketing his change, Peter said to Jake, "Have you heard from Adrian to say how much longer he is going to be?"

"He shouldn't be much longer, but I'll call him if you like."

"No, that's fine. We'll wait a little longer before troubling him. Meanwhile, can you remember what time our friend Dick arrived and left on Wednesday?"

"He was here when I arrived. I'm supposed to start at half past seven, but I was running late. Adrian told me he'd been waiting outside when he opened at eleven o'clock that morning. He asked me to keep an eye on him as he was starting to annoy the other customers. He said to call up the stairs for him if there was any trouble." Jake thought for a while before saying to one of the two men sat at the bar, "You were in then, weren't you, Bill?"

A grey-haired man dressed in mud-stained overalls stared intently into his drink as if it held all the answers to world peace. "Aye. 'E was becoming a bit much."

"In what way?" Peter asked.

"'E kept on asking where the wealthy, pretty women of a certain age lived in the area. The mature types 'e wanted." Bill took a gulp from his pewter tankard and nodded over to the corner. "I guess our Gladys was of the age 'e had in mind."

"Did you notice what time he left or whether he was watching for someone through the window?"

Bill stroked the grey stubble on his chin. "Reckon 'bout nine. But nay lad, 'e weren't lookin' out no window. Seven sheets to the wind 'e was by the time he left. 'E could hardly focus on puttin' one foot in front of t'other."

"Thanks for that, Bill. Can I buy you a drink?"

"Nah. You're alright, lad. Gotta be gettin' back to work anyhow."

Settled back around the table, keeping a wary eye on Colin who had fallen asleep under the table, Peter said hesitantly, "Gladys said you were an inmate with her brother in Shoreham prison?"

"I was indeed falsely imprisoned in that den of iniquity for many months while the wheels of justice slowly revolved. Eventually, common sense prevailed, and the unenlightened saw the error of their ways. While there, however, I was fortunate enough to make the acquaintance of some splendid fellows, plus of course the charming lady sitting before us in all her glory."

Peter gave Fiona an exasperated look and took a sip from his pint. Interrupting the flirtatious smiles Dick and Gladys were sharing, he cleared his throat and said, "Did these splendid fellows include Rob Creer?"

Dick raised his little finger as he took a delicate sip from his champagne flute. "I don't believe so."

Gladys nudged him in the ribs. "Oh, you silly thing. Did you mishear the name? I remember you telling me all about him. You told me last night about his little weenie."

"Oh yes, so I did," Dick agreed, his admiration of Gladys visibly waning.

"You do know Rob Creer," Peter said.

"Good Lord, young man! No, I do not. That man, and I'm interpreting that word most liberally, is a brute of the most terrible degree. Indeed, there is nothing splendid about that outrageous man at all. Just the suggestion is ludicrous." Dick banged his staff which had been resting on the side of the table, three times on the stone floor to emphasise his point. He leaned forward and added, "Even as I was preparing to leave that horrendous place, he continued to hound and taunt me. He said," Dick looked about the bar checking for prying eyes or anyone who might be listening. "He said, 'Don't get too comfortable. I'll see you on the outside shortly.' The way he said it, still sends shivers down my spine."

Gladys gasped and clutched Dick's arm. Looking around the bar herself she whispered, "You mean he's going to escape and hunt you down like an animal?"

Dick took both her hands in his. "Don't concern yourself, my good woman. I will protect you from the jaws of his evil." He extracted a hand to sip from his champagne flute. "In any event, he'll never find me. I'm avoiding my home town and touring the country in Bertha, so I won't be easy to locate."

"Where is your home town?" Fiona asked.

"The town of my birth is Brookeridge. My dear friend Bob moved away after his wife was murdered. I was wrongly accused of that murder, plus I was tricked out of my herbal remedies company by an evil witch, so there's nothing to entice me back there. If I was to return I would only become the focus of local titter-tattle."

"You poor dear!" Gladys said, rubbing his back. "How absolutely awful to feel you are unable to return to the town of your birth. You've suffered so much as a result of the mistakes of others. You must park Bertha out of sight in my garage and stay with me until the danger has passed." She turned her head to Peter. "Mustn't he, Peter? And shouldn't he have twenty-four-hour police protection after what he has been through?"

"Rob Creer is being held in a high-security prison. We spoke to them only this morning," Peter replied.

Gladys' hand shot to her mouth, and her eyes widened theatrically in horror. "Why would you be making enquiries of him at this time? Are you investigating the murder of that poor social worker in the woods?" She paused to catch her breath. "You are, aren't you and you think that dreadful man might be responsible? In that case. Dick must have our protection."

"Whoa there. You need to slow down, Gladys, and not let your imagination run away with you. We've checked, and he was in prison at the time, so he can't have murdered anyone," Fiona said.

"But for how long?" Dick said in a mysterious tone of voice, stroking his beard. "For how long?"

"Do you have evidence Rob Creer planned a prison escape?" Peter said abruptly.

"I've told you what he said to me as I was leaving. That is all I know about the matter. I can tell you he regularly boasted about how he was going to live like a king once he got out and recovered his ill-gotten gains. None of it was ever recovered, you know. Rumour has it that the total is between five and ten million. It's still out there somewhere," he said, looking into the distance with a dreamy look on his face. Returning his attention to the table, he added, "That amount of money could tempt a saint."

"I'm sure it could. And would you happen to know where it is hidden?" Peter asked.

"I must protest your insinuation," Gladys said in a loud voice. "Dick has no interest in material possessions. Isn't that right, Dick?"

"Of course, my darling they are of no concern to me. I have forsaken such petty trifles. The riches I seek are to be found on a far higher plane. You, my dearest, have had the benefit of hearing my views on many such matters. These good people do not know me as well as you do, so we must make allowances for their misinterpretations." Bowing to Gladys, he said, "I must however, take this opportunity to thank you for your gallant defence of my honour."

"Very touching. We could continue this conversation at the station," Peter said.

"Peter! How dare you speak to Dick that way!" Gladys exclaimed. "I should give you a clip around the earhole for being so presumptuous."

Peter dismissed Gladys with a wave of his hand. "Well, Dick, what can you tell me about this hidden hoard of treasure?"

"Very little. Nothing at all really. It's only gossip I overheard. Probably no truth in it at all."

"I'll be the judge of that. What do you know of the whereabouts of Creer's stash of money?"

"All I heard was that some of the stash is in diamonds and the rest is in cash."

"And where is it?" Peter asked.

"I have no idea. All I know is it is being kept safe by a trusted friend."

"It would have to be a very trustworthy friend to resist temptation and hold on to that amount of money for him. Any idea who this friend might be or where we would find him?"

"I believe you have misunderstood the relationship betwixt my good self and that rotten scoundrel. I was never his confidant. The ghastly bore ridiculed all that I stand for. Peace, compassion and living as one with the natural world. Her bounty provides riches enough for one such as I. As an honourable citizen I am merely passing on the little snatches of conversation I have overheard."

"And Vivien Morse? How well did you know her?"

"Really Peter! I must protest," Gladys interrupted.

Peter raised a hand to silence her but spoke directly to Dick, "Do you want to accompany us back to the station to answer these questions?"

Dick shook his head.

"We know Vivien was in here the same time as you on Wednesday, the evening she was attacked. So, I'll ask again, how well did you know her?"

Dick squirmed in his seat and drank the last of his champagne. "I over imbibed on that particular occasion, I'm ashamed to say, so I remember very little of the evening."

"I suggest you try a little harder to recall the events of that day. I'm meeting the landlord shortly who remembers both of you being in here, so I will find out. It would be better for you if you volunteered the information."

"I didn't want to draw attention to myself, but yes, I did recognise her from the picture in the newspaper. I had no previous knowledge of the good woman before that fateful day, and I can categorically state although I noticed her, I did not enter into any conversation with her or her friend. They were both too young and brash and didn't stay for very long. Indeed, they appeared to be in an intense disagreement and then both left."

"Together?"

"No. The lady in the newspaper left first. Her friend finished her drink and left about ten minutes later."

Peter looked directly into Dick's eyes and said, "And where was she when you left here?"

"I have no idea. The lane was empty as Colin led me to Bertha."

"Where did you go after?"

"Nowhere. I was in no fit state to drive, so I slept in Bertha in the car park until the break of dawn."

"I can vouch for that," a deep voice announced. "Although dawn was long gone by the time he left." A smartly dressed hulk of a man standing well over six foot with a broad muscular frame offered his hand to Peter. "I'm Adrian. Sorry to keep you waiting but I can confirm he is telling the truth. As a responsible landlord when I realised the inebriated state this gentleman was in I suggested he crawl into his camper van to sleep it off rather than attempt to drive anywhere."

Peter stood and shook Adrian's hand. Before leaving the table, he said to Dick, "Goodbye for now but we will wish to speak to you again Mr …"

"Dee-ath. Mr Richard Dee-ath at your service."

With her notebook in hand, Fiona asked, "How do you spell your surname?"

Dick spelt out, "D.E.A.T.H."

"Death?" Peter said. "Your surname is Death?"

"No, it's pronounced Dee-ath."

"In South Africa maybe. Here it is Death. We need to know where you are staying."

"With me of course," Gladys interrupted. "I'll take good care of him. Don't you worry about a thing. I'll keep him safely under my protection."

Adrian led Peter and Fiona behind the bar, along a corridor lined with boxes of bottled beer and crisps to a small office. The space was cramped and untidy. Adrian removed piles of invoices, receipts and trade magazines from three chairs. "Do sit down," he said, depositing the debris removed from the chairs in an untidy pile on the floor. "The lady who organises my accounts will be along later to sort this mess out, but we should have an hour of privacy before she arrives."

Peter handed the photograph of Vivien to Adrian. "Just to clarify. Is this the woman you saw in here on Wednesday?"

After a quick glance, Adrian nodded. "Without a doubt. I took notice of the two women for three very good reasons." He counted on his fingers, "One, I try to be welcoming to all new customers. Two, they were both rather attractive and three, they started to argue, and I had to ask them to keep their voices down."

"Did you catch what they were arguing about?"

"Sorry I just heard odd words like client and professional conduct. As they were both dressed smartly in office wear, I assumed it was a work-related disagreement."

"And did they quieten down?" Peter asked.

"The woman who was killed slammed down her unfinished drink and marched out in a huff. The other woman gave me an apologetic smile and moved over to a quiet corner to finish her drink. About ten to fifteen minutes later, she placed her empty glass on the bar, thanked me and left," Adrian said.

"Roughly what time was this?"

"I'd say they were in here between five o'clock and half-past, give or take a few minutes."

"Can you describe the other woman?" Peter asked.

"Very sharply dressed in a navy business suit. Brunette hair, lots of make-up and perfectly manicured nails I noticed as she handed over her glass. As long as they look over eighteen, I'm not good with ages. I'd guess they were of a similar age, mid-thirties possibly."

Fiona handed over her phone showing a promotional company photograph of Jane Salt. "Would this be the woman she argued with?"

Adrian took the phone and squinted at the screen. Handing it back he said, "I'm not totally sure, but yes I think that is her. Do you have a more natural looking picture I could look at?"

"We can arrange that later. Did you see the two women arrive or leave the car park?"

Adrian shook his head.

"Did you see the wayward Druid Dick out there talk to either of the women?"

"That oddball? No. He was as drunk as a skunk and starting to irritate some of my regulars. I'm fairly certain he didn't speak to the two ladies before they left. In hindsight, I should have asked him to leave before I went upstairs for my supper. But you know how it is. I expected him to be gone when I came back downstairs after a break. When I saw he was still propping up the bar, I escorted him to his van and told him not to drive anywhere until he'd sobered up."

"Did you notice what time he drove off?" Peter asked.

"The van was still parked in the same place when I took a beer delivery at about nine o'clock the next morning. I noticed with some relief it was gone when I opened up just before eleven."

"Did you actually see him at any point after you took him outside?"

"No, but the state he was in I would be very surprised if he left his van," Adrian said.

"Thank you. That's very helpful. Could you tell me who else was in the pub that night?"

"No one out of the ordinary. The usual local crowd."

"And the customers he annoyed?"

"Local horsey women who often dine in here. I would prefer it if they weren't hassled any more. I gave them a bottle of wine to apologise for his behaviour. They seemed to be okay about it, but competition is fierce around here. I don't want them to start going elsewhere."

"What exactly did he do?"

"Just being flirtatious and suggestive. Excuse the pun, but he was being a bit of a dick."

ELEVEN

Once clear of the Inn Peter said, "What did you make of that?"

With her phone already clasped in her hand, Fiona replied, "I take it you want me to get hold of Jane Salt."

"Yup. We're on our way to her workplace."

On the brow of the hill, Fiona said, "You're not going to like this. Today is her set day off in lieu of being on call over the weekend, and she's taken tomorrow off as well. It was booked weeks ago. I've tried her mobile and home phone, but she's not answering either."

"Goddamit!" Peter said, thumping his steering wheel. "Keep trying to get hold of her. We'll still head out to the offices. One of her colleagues may know where we could find her, plus they may be more inclined to talk to us without her around. In the unlikely event, she is able to give a perfectly acceptable reason for lying to us, we'll use this time to build as strong a case as possible against her for wasting police time if nothing else."

"Why do you think she did it?"

"Lied or battered her employee to death? We know only that she blatantly lied to us in failing to mention she met Vivien after her last call of the day. Don't forget, according to Adrian, Vivien left the Inn unharmed, and Jane made no attempt to rush out after her."

"Okay, why did she lie to us?" Fiona said. "And maybe we should also ask why Jane was so keen to direct our attention to the Bassett family, even referring to them as the last people to see her alive?"

"The argument in the pub sounded work-related. It is possible Vivian found out her boss had done something very wrong. That's my best bet for why Jane chose to lie to us, but that doesn't mean she attacked her."

"She struck me as the type of woman who'd do whatever it took to protect her position," Fiona said with conviction. "That would neatly explain the break-in at Vivien's home as well. Maybe Vivian discovered something that could lead to Jane losing her position if it came out. Jealousy is another possibility. Vivian was clearly a popular member of the team and despite her marital difficulties had a wide circle of friends outside of work. Should I arrange for Jane's home and car to be searched thoroughly?"

"You didn't like her very much, did you?" Peter said.

"No, she left me cold, but that's irrelevant. She lied to us and possibly broke into Vivien's house. Stokes said Vivien was dead by nine o'clock at the very latest. That's less than four hours after they argued."

"When we pull her in, we'll check her whereabouts earlier in the evening before she watched the barber of Fleet Street take his revenge. By the way, what was that you asked her about the actor's performance?"

"Oh yes," Fiona said, sitting back in the seat looking deflated. "I watched the same production of Sweeny Todd with Julien last week. My friend Sammie Ball is in the chorus, and she told me the actor who plays Pirelli has laryngitis. Wednesday was his last performance before the understudy took over. I guess Jane couldn't have been lying about watching the performance that evening." After some thought her face became animated. "She could have given her ticket to a friend and then called them to ask what they thought of the performance."

"We can check that," Peter said. "Any other ideas about why she chose not to mention she met Vivien after she left Ellen Bassett other than she was the killer?"

"Not off the top of my head," Fiona said.

"Vivien's attacker being female would explain why the only

clear footmarks they found at the scene were made by women's shoes. The assumption any marks made by a flat shoe were lost due to the wet ground conditions may be completely wrong," Peter said.

"Shame the landlord didn't overhear exactly what they were arguing about in the bar."

Although I said we wouldn't want the names of the other customers, it might be unavoidable," Peter said. "Until we have an explanation for the omission Jane is added to the list of serious suspects. And how about Gladys' friend, Dick? What did you make of him?"

Fiona chuckled and shook her head. "Totally bizarre, but by all accounts, he was paralytic and incapable of anything that night."

"Murder isn't a laughing matter."

"Sorry, sir, I agree, but you must admit it is very funny. Only Gladys could visit a high-security prison and leave with a Druid priest called Death."

In a deadpan tone, Peter replied, "That's what he is? I had wondered."

"They seemed very well matched as a couple. Maybe they'll get married, and Gladys will call herself something like Moonbeam."

"I doubt it. The female dog is called Colin," Peter said, shaking his head in mock despair.

Fiona couldn't hold back her laughter. With tears streaming down her face she repeated, "Colin? The female dog is called Colin?"

Peter nodded his head as Fiona tried to stop laughing. Suppressing a smile, he said, "Okay, okay, I admit the situation was somewhat unusual. Get it out of your system and then we'll talk sensibly about this. We are conducting a murder investigation and the arrival of Dick Death, humorous though it may be, is another consideration and yet another odd connection to Rob Creer. While Gladys is a rather annoying thorn in my backside at times, I don't want to see her hurt. I know the landlord said he was inebriated but he did see the two women arguing, and no one knows for sure he didn't leave his camper van."

"Why would Vivien have hung about the area after she stormed out unless it was to continue the argument with Jane?" Fiona said.

"Try her number again."

After trying both numbers, Fiona said, "Still no reply."

"Call the station and get her description and car registration number circulated. Hopefully, we'll be able to question her about the pub visit before the end of today."

"What about the millions Creer is supposed to have left with a friend? Do you think that may be the real reason Dick is here?"

"I think that's exactly why he is here, regardless of whether or not they were on friendly terms," Peter replied.

"Are you thinking Vivien may have been the trusted friend?"

Peter shrugged. "Apparently, she was very trusting."

❖ ❖ ❖

Their visit to Birstall was frustrating. Despite sharing knowing looks, the most any of the staff would admit to was sometimes there was friction between Jane and Vivien. Despite the seriousness of the situation, they refused to say more or give access to anything else without permission from someone superior. The only useful information they picked up was Jane Salt generally visited her ageing mother in an old people's home somewhere in Birmingham on her day off, and she often switched her mobile off on purpose. One employee thought she'd mentioned staying with an old college friend who had recently divorced but she couldn't remember the name or where the friend lived.

Leaving the office complex, no further forward, Peter felt his stomach rumbling. "Are you hungry? As we didn't end up eating earlier, I thought we could pop into The Horseshoe to grab something quick."

"Sure."

"As it's not that far away, the locals are bound to have an opinion on the Bassett family and Vivien's murder. Unless Jane Salt immediately rolls over and gives a full confession, I still think there are plenty of other avenues we should take a closer look at."

"Such as?

"The husband. Ian Bassett. The real reason our amorous Druid is in the area."

Fiona tapped Peter on the shoulder. "Don't set me off laughing again."

"Can we agree to only see the funny side of Dick after we've established he is harmless and not involved in any way? After her brother, we can't rely on Gladys' judgement. If he does stick around, I might just pull his file as I'd like to know a little bit more about his background and why he was looking through Mandy Lisle's cottage window."

The Horseshoe Inn was disappointingly quiet, and they learnt nothing new over lunch. Lorraine, the landlady, was only able to confirm the Bassett family kept themselves to themselves and she was pretty sure she'd never seen the daughter out and about by herself.

At the station, Peter tried to discover who he needed to contact to speed up getting full access to Jane Salt's work files while Fiona called Shoreham Prison.

"Well, that's annoying," Fiona said, replacing the receiver. "There is nobody currently available to say anything at all about prison visitors. They're going to ring me back later, and it was very much, 'Don't ring us, we'll ring you.' I got the impression I'm in for a long wait."

"Strange. Keep me posted on that. At this rate, I'm going to have to get the Super involved to get access to the records we need. We must clarify whether Jane has disappeared on purpose or is blissfully unaware of how much we want to speak to her and is busy celebrating her friend's divorce."

"Have you been able to find out which nursing home her mother is in?"

"You don't think I would have called them if I did?" Peter replied sharply. He walked to the whiteboard at the front of the room and drew a large circle around, 'Dick, the Druid.' Checking the clock, he said, "I'm going to go and have a word with the Super now. Have a flick through the details we have of Vivien's clients to see if there are any cases Jane also worked on."

Peter returned ten minutes later. "Wonderful. That's just wonderful. Our esteemed leader is out playing golf." Plonking himself in his chair, he said, "I may as well go through the files with you." Unused to spending an afternoon in the station reading reports, he soon felt tired and groggy. The constant mugs of coffee made him jittery but failed to inject any life into his weariness.

Fiona placed yet another mug of coffee on Peter's desk in the late afternoon and said, "According to Vivien's friends, they were all unaware of a significant boyfriend. It appears very odd that she would talk to a client about a boyfriend no one else has heard of."

Peter raised his head. "Yes, it does sound improbable. Which adds another puzzling question. A figment of a damaged girl's imagination or an attempt to misdirect us?"

"There's always the possibility Vivien really wanted to talk about her secret lover to someone and Ellen was a good choice, because if she ever mentioned anything, it could be explained away as the fantasy of a damaged mind?" Fiona suggested.

"Hardly the actions of a professional dealing with a vulnerable client."

Fiona shrugged. "Wasn't professionalism something the two of them were arguing about in the pub?"

"Not the kind of thing you'd expect to get killed for, though. The more I think about it, the less likely I think it is that Jane is our murderer." Peter rubbed his eyes. "Maybe a complaint was made about Vivien's lack of professionalism. Jane met her to discuss it, and Vivien stormed off to get attacked by a totally random stranger, and all this is a complete waste of time."

"If it were that way round, why would Jane have lied about meeting up with her?"

"If we keep digging, something will turn up," Peter said.

"Only if we're digging in the right places. Having spoken to Ellen, I'm not so sure we should take any notice of the suggestion of a boyfriend." Tapping the side of her head, she added, "To be honest I don't think she has enough going on upstairs. It really was like talking to a ten-year-old child."

"Ten-year-old children can be very advanced liars in my experience, or Vivien could have made the same assumption as us and said something in passing, thinking Ellen wasn't listening."

Peter stood and slowly moved to the whiteboard. "Although nothing has been found at his house and his alibi appears solid, I'm reluctant to completely forget about the husband, Nigel Morse." Underlining his name on the board, Peter said, "He remains an important suspect."

Drawing a circle around Ian Bassett's name, he continued, "This is despite the fact at the moment I can see no obvious reason for him to attack a woman who visited to help his daughter."

Next, he wrote Ellen Bassett. "The daughter is the only person who has claimed Vivien had a boyfriend. As she is not of sound mind, this suggestion may be a complete red herring or a more sinister attempt to distract us from the truth."

He then added Jane Salt to the board, underlining her name several times. "Fiona's hot favourite."

"Yes. She lied to us, she was seen arguing with the victim hours before she was attacked and has now disappeared. She specifically told us the Bassett family were the last people to see her alive," Fiona said.

Peter drew a line linking Dick the Druid to Creer with a huge question mark next to the name.

Fiona muttered something inaudible as Abbie Ward entered the room to place a file on Peter's desk. "What is that on the board about Dick the Druid?"

Peter grimaced. "We came across him today in the Bear and Ragged Staff Inn, which is almost the centre point between Park Farm and where Vivien's body was found. He was in the bar the same time as Vivien and has recently been released from Shoreham Prison."

Ward stared blankly at the board before handing over the file.

"Are you bringing this Dick character in for questioning?"

Peter said, "Fascinating as he may be, I'm only going to waste police time on the matter if we do find something to link him in with the murder. If I had time to waste I would bring him in on the Peeping Tom accusation. Unfortunately, I can't put him away for being an idiot."

"You've lost me there, sir?" Abbie said.

Peter waved away her comment. "Something of nothing and not my main concern. Fiona thinks she's solved the case, anyway, while I'm still on the starting blocks." Flicking through the file, he said to Abbie, "Thank you for your hard work today."

Abbie didn't leave the room as Peter had expected but started a conversation with Fiona. Peter tidied a few files on his desk and then picked up his jacket and keys. "Sorry to interrupt, but I'd like a quick word with Fiona before I leave." Taking her to one side, he said, "I'm going to pay Nigel Morse another visit to update him and might disappear home straight after. Until we know whether Jane Salt is dutifully visiting her mother or her friend and has a perfectly good explanation for why she didn't mention her meeting with Vivien, we're at a bit of an impasse with that angle. If anything else comes in, contact me at once."

"Will do." Fiona turned as though accepting the position. After taking a step, she spun around to face Peter. "Why don't you think her capable of murder?"

"I haven't said that. What I've said is, I can't see why a law-abiding professional woman would lure her employee into the woods and batter her to death. If you think differently, then convince me."

"She lied about meeting her in the pub," Fiona said.

"Yes, we do need to question her about that but bear in mind this heated discussion took place in a public place, and Vivien walked away unscathed. It might help if we knew what they were arguing about. It could be anything. Surely you can do better than that?"

"She would have access to Vivien's work schedule, she misdirected us about the Bassett family being the last people to see her, and there's a known tension between the two women. If Vivien discovered something like say, Jane having an inappropriate relationship with a young offender, that would destroy her career, and I think she would kill to prevent that happening," Fiona said.

"While I'm speaking to Nigel Morse, you find me a scrap of evidence that Ms Salt has acted improperly, and I'll look into it." Peter stopped in his tracks. "You've just given me an idea. What about Ian Bassett?"

"Sorry?" Fiona replied grumpily. "What about him?"

"What I was thinking was Ian Bassett might be the boyfriend, and that was what Jane and Vivien were arguing about. From the little we saw of the Bassetts, the marriage is not a happy one, and he was very on edge when we visited. Maybe he was seeing Vivien, and that would explain both the meeting in the pub away from the office and why Jane chose not to mention it. An employee having an affair with a client wouldn't reflect well on her as a manager. But it certainly wouldn't give rise to the need to silence her. She may have decided to keep quiet to protect Vivien's reputation."

Fiona shrugged. "It's a possibility."

"That's the point I'm trying to make here. Yes, Jane lied to us and it is annoying we haven't been able to speak with her to find out why, but we don't have sufficient grounds to call her a murderer. If you uncover a compelling reason for her to attack Vivien, then it would be a different matter. Thinking about my suggestion of an affair with Ian Bassett, what if the wife Lucy found out about it and then came across Vivien leaving the pub? We questioned her about her daughter leaving the house that evening but not her." Out of the corner of his eye, he spotted Abbie loitering by the door. "Sorry I interrupted your chat. I'm going to give the idea some thought this evening, and we'll go out to see the Bassett family tomorrow morning."

Fiona looked over at Abbie. "We were only discussing meeting up for a drink after work, she can wait. I want to know why it's okay for you to have hunches and gut feelings but not me."

"Whoa there. That's not what I've said. You haven't been listening. What I said is build me a convincing case to support your hunch, and we can look at it. Simply saying she lied isn't enough."

"That's not what it sounded like."

"I'm sorry if it sounded different to how I intended, and it has offended you. Have an enjoyable evening, and we'll discuss it properly tomorrow. Okay?"

Fiona's face was scarlet with anger when Abbie came over and said, "What's wrong?"

Aware her face was burning, Fiona turned her head and said, "Nothing really. Peter just irritated the hell out of me."

With a quizzical look, Abbie said, "You two normally get along really well. My shift is over, so I'm off home as well. You still set to come over tonight? We can bemoan the attributes of men all night long if it will cheer you up."

"Yes, I'll be around later. There are just a few things here I want to finish up before I leave."

TWELVE

Smarting from the childish spate with Fiona, Peter poked his head into reception to say goodnight to Sykes and ended up discussing the poor state of British football for ten minutes. A proper man-to-man conversation where you said what you meant without weird undercurrents of meaning.

On route to Nigel Morse's home, he pondered what was wrong with Fiona. Ian Jenkins' old DCI position would be advertised soon, and he was going to recommend her. He was only pushing to ensure she was ready, not trying to give her a hard time. Taking it so personally confused him. Her overreaction seemed, well off-kilter, and out of character. Or maybe it was just that special time of the month for her. At least when the twins grew up, he wouldn't be outnumbered by women at home. If his marriage managed to limp on for that long.

Finding a place to squeeze his car onto the pavement, he thought about Fiona's comment about clothes on their first visit. Walking past the row of identical houses, repeated for several streets, he dismissed the idea Nigel had money to burn. Nobody with excess cash would choose to live in such a drab place. Admittedly not the worst neighbourhood for crime, but not great either.

It was short-term accommodation. First-time buyers desperate to move away from overprotective parents and young couples who'd been caught out by unprotected sex were the main residents. Someone forced to find somewhere quick and cheap to rent until the divorce proceedings were finalised also fitted the demographics. By the time he reached the garden gate, he was convinced Fiona was mistaken. The suits she spotted were fake copies, good copies maybe, but fake all the same. No one choosing to live here would blow £1000 on one suit.

Nigel greeted him at the back door in faded jeans and a baggy sweatshirt. A smart dresser himself, Peter recognised at a glance these were the type of clothes picked up in a supermarket with the groceries. The type hung at the end of an aisle beneath a colourful handwritten sign shouting, 'Sale.'

While Nigel made coffee, Peter studied his slicked back hair. The colour was way too black to look natural. Any quality hairdresser would have chosen a subtler tone. By the time he had a mug of steaming coffee in his hand, Peter was sure it was a cheap home dye job. The kit picked up from the same supermarket aisle as the jeans. All of which discounted the likelihood of Fiona's supposed price tags on the suits. Nigel did not have that sort of money to spend on his appearance.

Remembering Mrs Morse's comment from earlier, Peter asked, "Do you have a dog?"

Nigel replied, "Sort of. A yappy little terrier. The neighbours are always complaining about the noise he makes if he's left alone on an evening. I reckon one of them left the back gate open on purpose to spite me and he has wandered off. No doubt he'll come back in his own good time. Viv doted on him, but he's the type of dog that can look after itself."

Nigel led him from the kitchen, through the lounge area to a small dining room table with four chairs. Spread across the table were several books claiming to make the reader an overnight sales sensation. All that was needed was a little positive-thinking.

Peter picked up a glossy brochure half tucked away under the sales books titled,
'Thinking of working in America?' and flicked through it. "Planning on moving abroad?"

Nigel reached to take the brochure from him. His sleeve pulled back to reveal a gold Rolex watch, which glinted under the overhead light. "Something I'm considering. You know a fresh start. If I don't do it now when I have no responsibilities, I never will. I had planned on working abroad after college, but I was already with Viv, so it never happened. Don't worry, looking at all the hoops I must jump through first, it won't be any time soon. And that's assuming I can find a job over there. Chances are it won't happen at all. Dreaming about the prospect takes my mind off things." He neatly piled the remaining books and asked, "Am I still a suspect?"

Peter dodged a direct reply by saying, "You've not been eliminated yet. I'm here to clarify a few things about your stop at the motorway services."

"I'm not sure I can add anything more to my original statement, but I'm happy to run through it again if it will help. Traffic had been heavy but moving albeit at a sedate pace. It had been raining on and off all day and started getting dark a little after three. Sales wise I'd had a good day. I hadn't slept well the night before, and I'd been caught by heavy showers a couple of times, which along with my marital problems, made me feel down and weary. Worried I might drop off to sleep at the wheel, I thought rather than rushing to get back to the office I should stop off to get a strong coffee and some fresh air. I pulled into the services a little after five o'clock and stayed for about an hour."

"Where did you get your coffee?"

"As I said in my statement, at the Costa shop. I sat by the window watching the rain and reading a newspaper left on the table by an earlier customer. It was too wet to take a walk outside to clear my head. I wandered about inside, played a slot machine for a while and then looked at some ties in the Tie Rack shop. After that, I visited the newsagents. I used the bathroom, bought another Costa coffee and returned to my car to drive the rest of the way home. I understand the customers I chatted with in the Willy Wicket pub have confirmed I was there the rest of the evening."

"And yet none of the staff working at the service station that day remembers seeing you," Peter said.

"They must serve hundreds of strangers, just passing through every day." Nigel shrugged. "If the boot was on the other foot and you asked me to identify the people who served me, I wouldn't be able to pick them out of an identity parade. I was feeling pretty glum at the time. I queued up with strangers and handed my money over. It wasn't a memorable encounter. I wish I hadn't thrown my receipts into the bin, but I did. I wasn't expecting to have to prove my whereabouts. If I was on the way to kill my wife, I'm pretty damn sure I would have held on to those receipts."

"How did Vivian get along with Jane Salt?"

"I'm quite sure that cold-hearted bitch hasn't had a good word to say about me. I'm equally sure she encouraged Vivian to seek a divorce," Nigel said.

"They were friendly?"

"Civil and polite, rather than cosy and friendly."

"But they got along? No personal or work-related frictions?"

"As far as I'm aware they got along fine. Vivien didn't talk about her work at home. My guess would be old Frosty Lips liked her a lot more when she was ditching me. I never liked the woman. Even at college, she had a reputation for being a prick tease and a stuck-up snob," Nigel said.

"Earlier I noticed you're wearing a rather nice watch. Rolex isn't it?"

Nigel blushed and pulled his left sleeve down. "I know technically it is wrong, and they are all rip-off fakes, but everyone buys the stuff down the market. As a single guy, I thought I could do with a bit of bling." He ran his hand through his hair and chewed his bottom lip. "Sorry to sound so glib. It's my way of coping. Everyone knows we were divorcing, but that doesn't mean I don't care. I just … It's difficult." He took a deep breath and pasted on a weak smile. "Retail therapy doesn't only work for the girls."

"When is the funeral?" Peter asked.

"Her family have taken over. It's organised for next Tuesday back up in Birmingham. If my name was taken off the suspect list by then, I'd be able to attend without being spat at. I'd be happy to stand at the back. I don't want to cause trouble, but I really would like to pay my respects. Our marriage may have ended badly, but we had some good times together."

"I'll see what I can do."

"If only she'd found a different line of work. You know it's not just those death-row prisoners in America that have millions of female pen pals and end up getting married in prison. Some of them do it over here as well. Can't see the attraction myself in exchanging letters with a mass murderer, but I guess it takes all sorts. I accept I'm not perfect, but I'd like to think I have more going for me than a convicted criminal."

"Did Vivien ever mention visiting a prisoner called Rob Creer?"

"She knew how I felt about the prison visits, so didn't mention any details to me. Certainly not individual names."

Peter stood. "Don't get up. I'll see myself out." He turned by the doorway and added, "I think I might visit Birstall market over the weekend to see if I can find myself a new watch."

◆ ◆ ◆

Peter opened his front door to the comforting smell of baking and laughter coming from the kitchen. He entered the room, and the sounds died away. "Don't mind me," he said into the uncomfortable silence. "I'll just grab a glass and get out of your way." He stretched to reach a brandy glass from the top cupboard.

"That bad a day?" Amelia, his daughter asked, bending to open the oven door.

Peter's partner Sally was leaning against a worktop on the far side of the room. He couldn't decipher the look on her face. He gave her an awkward smile. "Cold, wet and miserable. I need something to warm me from the inside." He caught the look of disapproval as Sally checked the time on her wristwatch. The desire to rebel clashed with his acceptance it was a tad early for the hard stuff. Rebellion won, and he poured himself a generous double.

Amelia placed a golden sponge cake on a tray to cool. "I'm cooking for you tonight. I could make your old favourite, sausage casserole. I'll add a little something to spice it up."

Peter glanced at Sally. Was it possible her dalliance with veganism was over? The bowl of soaking lentils on the counter suggested otherwise, but he could still hope.

"I'm eating out this evening," Sally explained. "There's a new Mexican in Birstall I want to try. I knew it wouldn't be your thing."

"Oh okay," Peter said, rolling the brandy around in the glass, no longer sure he wanted to start drinking so early in the evening. He took a small sip before placing it on the side. "Where are Liam and Thomas?"

"At a sleepover. I'll be free of those rascals until tomorrow lunchtime."

Peter took another sip of brandy. It was the first time Sally had ever said anything vaguely negative about the twins, even in jest.

"Sorry, Dad, you're stuck home alone with me tonight," Amelia said.

Before Peter could reply, Sally checked her watch again and made her way towards the door. "I'd best get a move on and get ready, or I'll be late."

"Do you need a lift anywhere?" Peter asked. "I've only had a couple of sips."

"Thank you, but it's all arranged. And don't wait up. I might be late home," Sally replied, closing the door behind her.

Peter stared at the door, unsure about what had just passed between them. Whatever it was he didn't like it. Although things had been sliding south for a while, he wasn't ready to lose her. Not without a fight anyway. Maybe he should have planned his campaign months earlier. Before she started living a separate life and telling him not to wait up for her.

"Dad? Hello. Amelia to planet Dad. Can you hear me?"

"Yes. Sorry I was miles away."

"Sausage casserole or something else?" Amelia deposited a heavy hardback cook book in his hands. "You decide."

"That will be perfect," Peter replied, handing the book back without looking at it. "I want a quick word with Sally before she leaves." He stopped abruptly in the doorway. "What were the two of you talking about when I came in?"

Amelia laughed. "First crushes."

"Oh. Who was Sally's?"

Looking at him as if he were stupid, Amelia replied, "After David Bowie, you."

Peter sat on the edge of their bed watching Sally apply her makeup at the dressing room table.

She put down her mascara wand and started to brush her hair. Looking at Peter's reflection in the mirror she said, "Do you have a problem with me going out?"

Peter replied to her reflection, "Of course not. I was just taken by surprise. If you'd said you wanted to go to a new restaurant, I would have taken you."

Continuing to brush her hair with long deliberate strokes she said, "No we would have talked about it, you would have said I don't like foreign food and we'd have arranged to go to a nice cosy pub somewhere. Only we wouldn't actually make it there. Something far more important would have come up, and you would have cancelled." She put down her brush. "No, not cancelled, postponed indefinitely which amounts to the same thing. Happens every time."

"Not every time."

"Nearly every time," Sally conceded. "The boys' sleepover came up, and I was chatting to Ruth about how I never go out anymore, and we arranged it. A spur of the moment thing."

"Is our age difference starting to bother you?" The shrill sound of Peter's mobile came from downstairs. "Amelia," Peter shouted through the open bedroom door and down the stairs. "Can you answer my phone and tell whoever it is I'm busy and will ring them back later."

Sally swung round on the stool. "No, it has nothing to do with you being older. I'd prefer to go out somewhere with you, but it just doesn't happen. I need to get out of here to have fun and have an adult conversation once in a while. Even when you're here, your mind is often elsewhere."

"Dad," Amelia called up the stairs. "It's Fiona Williams. Says it's important."

"Tell her I'll call her back," Peter shouted. He felt the barrier reappearing between them. Sally gave a sad, 'told you so,' smile and turned to face her reflection to attach her earrings. They were back to using the mirror as a go-between. Noticing how tightly Sally gripped her hairbrush when she picked it up, Peter said, "Our relationship is purely professional."

Without taking her eyes from her own reflection, Sally continued to brush her hair. "She's a very pretty girl."

Pushing away the memory of how close he'd come to crossing the line with Fiona, Peter replied. "She's a colleague. It's just work."

Sally put down the brush and studied his eyes in the mirror. "I know, but that's the point. It's not just work. It's who you are. Fiona shares a part of you I have no access to."

"Dad!" Amelia shouted.

The connection through the mirror was broken.

Peter asked, "Is it only you and Ruth going?"

Rearranging perfume bottles, Sally said, "Plus a few others. We're going on to a casino afterwards."

Peter knew several officers went to the casinos after late shifts. It was something that had never appealed to him. A vision of a James Bond type in a dinner jacket whisking Sally away to his yacht docked in the harbourside for cocktails appeared in his mind.

"Dad! She says you're really going to want to know about this."

"Go and take your call, Peter. I need to get dressed now," Sally said, walking around him to take an electric blue dress he didn't recognise from the wardrobe.

"Is that new?" Peter asked.

Sally returned to the stool and checked her makeup in the mirror. "Yes. I bought it today."

"It's pretty." Reluctantly Peter stood. He hesitated before kissing Sally on the top of her head while watching her reflection in the mirror. "Have a lovely evening."

"Dad!" Amelia shouted, impatiently.

"Take your call, put on your superman outfit and go and save the world," Sally said, avoiding eye contact.

Peter gave Sally a final squeeze of her shoulder. From the top of the stairs, he shouted, "Okay! I'm coming down now."

He took the phone from Amelia and said, "This had better be important."

Disconnecting the call, he went in search of Amelia in the Kitchen. "Sorry, we're going to have to take a rain check on that casserole. I'm needed back at the station." Already halfway into his jacket, he added, "I shouldn't be long. A couple of hours tops."

THIRTEEN

Peter had to knock three times on the front door to Gladys' cottage before the loud classical music playing inside was turned down. The crash of symbols had contrasted sharply with the uncomfortable silence between Peter and Fiona. Waiting for the door to be answered over the din, he considered how best to apologise for shouting at her. It was hardly her fault the prison decided just that moment to come clean and contact her to admit Rob Creer had escaped their facility. But still, the timing of her call rankled him.

The door was flung wide open, and the hall light silhouetted Gladys from behind. Gladys in full ball gown, high heels and long white gloves was a sight to behold. Beneath her makeup, some of which was starting to melt and slide downwards, her face glowed bright red. Her grey hair had at some point earlier in the evening been piled high upon her head. Strands with pins still attached were making a hasty escape, fleeing in all directions. A bead of sweat ran down the bridge of her nose as she panted in the doorway, trying to catch her breath.

"Gladys is your friend Dick with you?" Peter asked.

Holding her ample figure up with the assistance of the door, Gladys managed a brief nod. The ability to speak as her chest heaved appeared beyond her.

"May we come in?"

Gladys nodded before moving aside and beckoning them inside. When she turned to face them, her breathing was slowly returning to normal. "Darlings, how perfectly divine to see you both," she said breathlessly, air-kissing them on both cheeks. "What brings you out on this enchanted evening?" Her face darkened at the sight of their stern faces and before either of them could reply she added, "Good heavens above! It is only nine o'clock, and the music wasn't that loud. Which one of the miserable old bats complained? They're only jealous, you know." She reopened the door and stuck her head out into the lane and shouted, "Old before their time, the whole lot of them."

"Come inside, Gladys. Nobody has complained about the music, although it was a little loud. We need to talk to you and Dick about something quite different," Peter said.

Gladys shut the door and twirled herself around. "It has to be loud enough to be felt," she said with a wave of her hand. "Have you ever given your soul over to the rhythm of the beat, Peter?"

"Not recently," Peter replied, cringing at the familiar use of his first name. He peered down the narrow hallway.

"Is Dick here?"

"Oh yes! He's been showing me his rhumba and cha-cha-cha. They're rather spectacular!"

"I'll take your word for it," Peter said, making his way along the corridor. He stopped with his hand on the knob of the nearest door. "This one?"

"Next one along, darling." Gladys turned to Fiona, "My dear, you really must introduce him to the passion of the tango. Explode all that awful tension he carries around with him into something simply wonderful."

Fiona indicated they should follow Peter. "I'll certainly suggest it to him."

Gladys pulled her to one side. "Is he not getting enough? Looks like a clear case of sexual frustration to me. Why don't you be an absolute poppet and help him out in that department? I sense you would like to."

"Really, Gladys. That's none of your business," Fiona said, brushing her aside.

The furniture in the living room had been moved to the sides to increase the dancing space. Dick was sitting cross-legged in the centre of the room, reverently stroking the covers of old LPs. Colin, the dog, raised her head from where she was curled up in the corner and gave a heavy sigh. After giving the new arrivals the once over she lowered her head back onto her front paws and closed her eyes.

"You and me both," Peter muttered.

At the sound of Peter's mumbled comment, Dick looked up. Clambering ungracefully to his feet, Dick offered his hand. "To what do we owe this great pleasure?" Gripping hold of Peter's hand, he shook it vigorously. "Do you enjoy a waltz of an evening with your good lady?"

Peter was temporarily struck dumb by the sight of a huge flower tucked behind Dick's ear.

Dick clapped his hands three times and danced a jig when Fiona entered the room. She came to a stop next to Peter while Dick bowed almost to the floor in front of her. Completing his low bow, he reached for Fiona's hand and kissed it. "My good lady. Would you and your partner care to join us in a quartet?"

"No, we're here in an official capacity. Would you please both sit down?" Peter said.

Dick and Gladys obediently plonked themselves down side by side on the sofa along the far side of the wall. Fiona and Peter pushed an armchair each into the centre of the room, facing the sofa.

Taking his seat, Peter said, "And take that flower out from behind your ear."

Dick obediently removed it while Gladys defiantly picked up a feather boa from the sofa and flung it dramatically around her neck. "My dear young man, you really are at risk of becoming an old fuddy-duddy in slippers with a pipe and a perfectly dreadful bore," Gladys said, before sticking out her tongue at Peter.

Peter gave her a hard stare. "The reason we're here is to tell you Rob Creer escaped from Shoreham Prison earlier today…"

"Good gracious!" Gladys screeched, jumped to her feet and ran for the door. "I must secure my property!"

The colour drained from Dick's face. "Do you think he's heading this way?"

"I was hoping you were going to tell us how likely that is," Peter replied. "When we met earlier, you told us he indicated he would be meeting up with you and that he has a friend keeping his money and diamonds safe for him to collect."

Dick pulled out a handkerchief and mopped a bead of sweat from his brow. "I was only repeating gossip. I thought it was an idle threat to scare me. I had as little as possible to do with the horrid little bully. You can ask anyone. We certainly weren't friends."

"I can check with the prison authorities, but of course an outward show of antagonism could have been just that. A pretence to cover up that you were, in fact, working together and had this all planned out."

"You've lost me. Planned what?" Dick replied with his arms outstretched.

"You to come down here before him and collect the cash and diamonds from Vivien Morse on Creer's behalf. Was Vivien the trusted friend? Did something go wrong when you accosted her? Maybe you were thinking of collecting the money for yourself and scarpering without waiting for Creer to escape and join you?"

"My good man! I have never in my life heard such preposterous nonsense. I have no idea of whom it is you speak."

"Oh, I think you do," Peter said.

Gladys rushed back into the room. "Whew! The chain is on, and all the bolts are drawn across. Will you be positioning armed policeman outside to protect us from this escaped villain?"

Peter rubbed his chin thoughtfully as Gladys cuddled next to Dick on the sofa. "I was thinking it might be best if Dick returns with us to the station." He held eye contact with Dick before continuing, "It would be easier for us to keep a close eye on him there. I'm sure he wouldn't want to place you in any danger. Am I right, Dick?"

"The last time I helped the police I ended up wrongly charged with the murder of my best friend's wife, so I'm not awfully keen."

"When did you arrive in the area, Dick?" Peter asked.

"A couple of weeks ago. Why?"

"Just before Vivien Morse suffered a break-in. Was that you?"

Fiona turned her face to Peter and spoke quietly so only he could hear. "Do you remember Vivien claimed there were dog hairs left behind?"

"When you couldn't find what you were looking for in the house, you spotted her in the pub."

"Have you lost your mind, dear fellow? I have no idea what you are talking about, and I most definitely did not break in and steal anything from the poor woman. I really must protest my innocence," Dick said.

"And why were you peering into a cottage window earlier in the week?"

"I most certainly was not."

"We could see if the woman who owns the cottage can identify you."

"This is outrageous," Dick replied, becoming increasingly red in the face.

"Put it this way. I could arrest you under suspicion of being a Peeping Tom, burglary and murder, or you could come voluntarily to the station to answer a few questions."

"Well, since you put it like that, maybe it would be for the best," Dick replied sarcastically. He twisted towards Gladys and took both of her hands in his. "There is not a word of truth in these ludicrous lies, but it may be for the best if I do as requested. Just for the time being, my little pumpkin. While I convince these nincompoops of my complete and total innocence." Dick disentangled himself from Gladys and stood. "Parting is such sweet sorrow."

Gladys reached for him. "I can hardly bear it, my love."

Dick beat his chest with his right fist. "We must stay strong, my lovely." He took a step towards Peter. "I am humbly at your service and put my well-being in the capable hands of the police service yet again. Only this time I trust I will be treated better."

"Someone will be out to collect your vehicle. Do you have the keys?" Taking the keys from Dick, Peter led him to the front door. Gladys burst into tears, pushed past them and fled upstairs.

FOURTEEN

Rob threw a lit match onto the small pile of tinder he'd built. He watched the small flames splutter then catch on the scrunched-up pieces of paper before they started to lick greedily at the small twigs. Mesmerised, he lost track of time as the fire crackled and danced. He was jolted from the simplicity of complete blankness when a chunk of wood dislodged and shifted, sending small red sparks into the air. He tracked the pinpricks of fiery light as they floated free, experiencing one last gasp of energy before falling to the ground as grey dust.

He reached inside his jacket pocket and pulled out a bundle of letters. He flicked off the elastic band and pulled a sheet of paper from one of the envelopes and read the first few lines.

"My darling Robbie, last night, I dreamt again of us being together. When I awoke, I could still feel your powerful protective arms around me and smell your scent. You are everything to me. Your soul calls to mine. We are destined to be joined as one."

Rob pushed the letter back in the envelope and raised the scented bundle to his nose before chucking the pile into the flames. As they crumpled in the heat, he pulled a second collection of letters from his jacket. He picked one at random.

"Hey Robbie, want to know what I'm wearing? I'm handcuffed to the bed writhing in anticipation of you. Hurry baby. I can't hold back much longer."

Rob threw his head back and laughed. "Oh, you are a naughty girl," he said, as the letters fluttered towards the flames.

He pulled out a third pile of letters.

"My darling Heathcliffe. You are the reason I breathe. Every day without you by my side is cruel torture."

These he kissed before slipping them back inside his jacket pocket. Patting his pocket, he said, "You will always have a special part in my heart, my little Jezebel. You've always thought yourself so classy and a cut above all the rest. Don't you know the mundane reality never lives up to the imagined expectations? Sooner or later you'll end up in the fires of hell with the rest. But for now, I'll spare you the indignity of being just another one, the same as all the rest." He stamped on the small fire to ensure the flames were fully extinguished before turning away.

Once he moved away from the fire the cold, damp air sent a shiver through him. He thrust his hands deep into his pockets as he watched the bleak day turn prematurely to night. His dismal surroundings reminded him of a water-colour artist's palette of browns and greys. The only relief came from blue pheasant feeder bins. Their artificial sheen emphasised that the foreign birds were imported to give a false display of sportsmanship. From the bins the birds were overfed so when they heaved their heavy bodies from the ground and struggled into flight, wealthy gentlemen would be able to shoot them down.

The musty smell of damp fallen leaves assaulted his nostrils but at least it silenced his footfall. A rustling sound to his right sent him diving for cover. His injured right leg ached and trembled as it started to spasm while he crouched behind a tree. He ignored the shooting pains and remained motionless on high alert, his eyes straining to see into the murky near-darkness. A flicker of doubt entered his mind only to be dismissed by his confidence. She was too in love with him to double cross him. It was possible she'd disobeyed his insistence that she keep her distance until they were ready to flee this damp, miserable country forever. Well, he was, anyway, once he'd recovered what was his.

From out of a thicket a deer emerged into the gloom of the evening, her vaporised breath creating a halo around her head. Startled by his presence, she turned and disappeared as swiftly as she'd appeared. Rob laughed out loud as he stood. His laughter sounded hollow as it echoed through the desolate scene. He stumbled and winced in pain as his leg threatened to give way underneath him as he pulled himself upright. Once he was gone from this godforsaken place where it always rained and spent his days in the hot Mediterranean sun, his mangled leg would heal. There would be plenty of hot senoritas to massage his calves with oil. His growing hard-on made it even more uncomfortable as he limped his away along the path.

He came to a fork in the path and swore. The stupid bitch didn't mention a fork. He crossed his fingers and took the right fork as the light drizzle that had hung in the air all day turned to persistent rain. The decomposing leaves that covered the track quickly turned to mush. As more water fell, the pre-existing puddles ran into one another making it impossible to step over them. His boots became waterlogged and squelched with each step. The rain turned to a torrential downpour that soaked through the light jacket he wore.

He was drenched to his underwear and shivering when the path narrowed to a dead end. His anger warmed him as he made his way back along the path which resembled a river as rivulets of water formed and streamed over his boots. Cursing with every step, he lowered his head and stomped along. "I'll kill her with my bare hands when I see her."

A fierce wind rattled through the trees, driving the relentless rain and lashing the skin of his face. An owl hooted in the distance as he trudged back along the track, hoping he was heading towards the cottage that had been rented for him. The only bonus was his face was turning so numb, he no longer felt the biting cold wind tearing at his exposed skin.

When it at last appeared, the tiny two bedroomed cottage nearly brought tears of relief to his eyes. His leg was screaming in protest as the dampness of the air mixed with his cold sweat. By the time he pushed the trailing ivy aside and finally lined his key up with the lock, his body ached all over, and he could no longer control his chattering teeth. It took a hard shove with his hip to dislodge the door from its warped frame.

Once inside he grabbed a bottle of whisky from the side bar and a packet of pills he found in a drawer. He drank from the bottle as he slumped onto a kitchen chair. He rested his foot on another chair as he gingerly pulled up his trouser leg and examined the fresh blood staining the dressing.

Unwrapping the soiled bandage, he tentatively poked the re-opened wound, causing pus to seep out. Worried about infection, he poured a generous amount of whisky over it. It stung like hell, causing his eyes to smart and he quickly decided the pain killing effects of drinking the contents a far better idea.

Carrying the bottle, he limped to a rocking chair in the corner of the snug living room. He covered himself in the blanket neatly folded on the back of the chair, took a long swig from the bottle and settled down for the night, waiting for oblivion to overtake him.

Rob struggled in his nightmare to free himself from the thick rope that tied him to the chair. The bindings so tight that his extremities tingled and sent electric shocks through his body as the blood supply slowed. In front of him, a huge stag danced on its hind legs to the tune a Druid priest played on his wooden flute. Wisps of memory of the scent his mother used to wear floated around his head mocking him as a hooded figure continued to drill a hole through his head. Rob felt the top of his head being sucked ever upwards. He scrambled to free his feet. If only he could reach the floor, he could raise himself higher to reduce the agonising pain the suction caused. A belching sound filled his eardrums. So loud he scrunched his eyes tight shut as though that would somehow reduce his overall reception of the excruciating agony. The noise rescinded, and he wished he'd not opened his eyes. His bloodied brain sat in the palm of an outstretched hand before him.

"Wake up, Robbie. Please wake up. It's me." Jane stared at the thermometer in horror. "Your temperature is through the roof." She grabbed her handbag and frantically searched through it. With relief, she pulled out a bottle of painkillers she'd been prescribed for back pain and a tab of over the counter tablets designed to reduce swelling and temperature. They wouldn't be enough, but they'd buy her some time before she could get some antibiotics. The rancid stench of rotting flesh from the leg wound almost overpowered her as she leaned down to inspect the dirty bandage. She toppled backwards, nearly falling, and staggered to the sink for a glass of water.

Returning to the chair, she shook Rob fiercely. Fear constricted her vocal chords, turning her voice to a high-pitched squeak. "Robbie!" she screamed hysterically. "For the love of God please wake up."

FIFTEEN

Peter updated the team on the overnight developments. They'd gone around in circles for hours interviewing Dick, and Peter felt tired and irritable. He was convinced Dick was lying to them and was in the area to look for something, almost definitely Creer's treasure. He couldn't even threaten him with a prosecution for being a Peeping Tom as Mandy Lisle had insisted she didn't want to make a fuss or press charges. The whiteboard showed he'd added a new suspect each day without eliminating anyone.

"Smith and Humphries, this morning I want you to visit Nigel Morse at work and let me know how he reacts. If he does one thing out of the ordinary, I want to know about it. While you're there, get a good look at his watch and then get yourselves out to Birstall market where he says he bought it. It looked like the real thing to me. If they're that good, I'd like one for my birthday. Before you leave, check on how they're getting on with the search of Dick's camper van that was brought in last night. If they haven't started yet, tell them it's urgent. Also, pull out the file on the break-in at Vivien's house and check if anyone had the foresight to hold on to some of the mysterious dog hairs. If they did, I want to see if they're from Dick's dog. Chances are the van is covered with them."

Peter turned to Litten and Ward. "Until I tell you differently, I want you to carry on working through Vivien Morse's client list, speaking to all of them, and flag anything of interest or concern for my attention. Before you start on the list, I want one of you to liaise with Shoreham Prison authorities and the local police searching for Rob Creer. Contact me the second he is recaptured or if there are definite sightings of him elsewhere. If he stays in the Midlands, we'll be able to discount him as an odd coincidence."

Over the noise of chair legs scraping along the floor as they were vacated, Peter said, "In response to the two media appeals no one has come forward to say they saw Vivien after she stormed out of The Bear and Ragged Staff Inn. To be fair, it is an isolated area, and the weather was atrocious, but if anyone should hear anything different, please contact me or Fiona immediately."

Abbie Ward stopped and asked, "Did any of the pub's other customers see her leave?"

"We haven't had the chance to check yet, but it is something I intend to follow up on later today."

Driving to Bassett's farm, Peter said, "Bright girl that Abbie. She's always the one who asks the intelligent questions. You're friendly with her. Any ideas of her future plans career-wise?"

"Not sure," Fiona replied. "She did mention wanting to work her way up through the detective ranks, but that was when Nick Tattner was taking his exams. I don't think I've heard her mention anything since."

Peter visibly flinched at the memory. "I might not talk about what happened, but I've not forgotten about him. He had a great future ahead of him. I don't think I'll ever stop feeling guilty over what happened."

"Sorry for bringing it up. You shouldn't feel guilty, though. It was hardly your fault."

"Maybe," Peter replied, in a way that indicated he felt there was no maybe about the subject.

"Anyway," Fiona said quickly. "I'm not sure Abbie is speaking to me. I was supposed to be going around hers last night, but with the prison escape and everything, I completely forgot. I only remembered when I literally bumped into her this morning. I don't think she was very impressed."

Peter gave her a quick glance as he pulled up outside Park Farm. "Go careful, you don't want to end up as irresponsible and thoughtless as I'm told I am on a regular basis." He watched Fiona roll her eyes before climbing out of the car. Peter climbed out and leaned over the car roof. "Who did you telephone last night then? Before we interviewed Dick, I overheard you apologising to someone, saying you were held up at work."

Fiona blushed and turned away towards the house. "Oh yes. That was Julien. Like I said, I'd completely forgotten I'd agreed to meet up with Abbie."

Catching up with Fiona on the garden path, Peter said, "Julien? That's the new boyfriend?"

Fiona pressed hard on the doorbell. "Yes."

Lucy Bassett opened the door in a coffee-stained dressing gown tied tightly around her middle and a burning cigarette in one hand. Her hair was tangled, and the red marks on her right cheek suggested they'd woken her up. After a short delay, Lucy's look of confusion changed to one of recognition. Her eyes slowly focused on them. "Back again? I thought we answered all your questions the last time you came here and disrupted our lives." She sucked hard on her cigarette, hollowing her cheeks, which instantly aged her by ten years. "I hope you're not here to hassle Ellen. It will mess up her routine all over again, and it's me that's left to pick up the pieces each time."

Peter flashed one of his charming smiles. "I appreciate that and will bear it in mind, but first it is you and your husband, Ian, we want to talk to. Is he in?"

Lucy flicked her cigarette stub out the front door and folded her arms. "What do you want with him?"

Peter kept his smile in place. "We just want to check a few things with him. Is he here?"

Lucy screwed up her nose and sniffed loudly. "Nope."

"Do you know where we could find him or when he'll be back?"

Lucy pulled a fresh cigarette from her pocket and lit it, inhaling deeply before stepping back into the corridor. Smoke curled from her nose while she eyed them suspiciously. "He generally pops in for a coffee and a snack about now. You'd best come in and wait." She led them into a spacious kitchen with glorious views across rolling countryside. Plonking mugs of coffee on the solid table top in front of them, she retrieved a bottle of brandy from the side. She poured a generous measure into her mug before offering the bottle around.

"Not for us, thanks," Peter said.

Returning the bottle to the counter, Lucy said, "Been a hard morning. I heard on the radio he escaped. He didn't just damage our little girl, you know. He sucked the joy out of all of us. We're hollow shells just going through the motions. Dragging ourselves through one miserable day after another." She took a gulp from her coffee mug and stubbed her cigarette out into an overflowing ashtray before lowering herself onto a chair. "If they don't get him back inside, there's no telling what our Ian might do. He'll go after him, I reckon, and there won't be a damn thing I can do to stop him. I dread to think what he'll do if he gets his hands on him. It won't be pretty, that's for sure."

"That really wouldn't be advisable, Mrs Bassett," Fiona said.

Lucy placed her elbows on the table and rested her chin on her cupped palms. "Like I have any control over what he does these days. Could you lock him up for his own good until they recapture Creer?"

"That's quite an unusual and extreme request," Peter said. "Do you think he represents a danger to the public?"

Lucy threw back her head and cackled. "No. Only to himself and that Creer monster."

"How about to you and Ellen?" Fiona asked.

"He'd never harm a hair on Ellen's head. He idolises her. Always has from the second she was born. Even now he won't stand any criticism of her or suggestion she's not quite right. He believes she'll get better. That all she needs is more time to heal and forget."

"Going back to Wednesday," Peter said. "The day of Vivien Morse's last visit. You told us Ellen didn't leave the house, but how about you? Did you go anywhere?"

Lucy shook her head. "Ian was out working, and Kathy wasn't around that day. I can't leave this prison when there is no one about to keep an eye on Ellen. Just in case she has one of her turns."

"What happens during her turns? Does she become violent?" Fiona asked.

"Sometimes." Lucy shrugged. "Other times she merely screams and throws things around. She smashed all the downstairs windows once for no obvious reason other than she felt bored." Lucy got up to take a fresh packet of cigarettes from a side drawer. Unwrapping the cellophane, she brightened slightly and added, "She's been a lot better since she started her new medication but I'm still reluctant to leave her alone."

"But there's no one to confirm the two of you remained on the property all night after Vivien left?" Peter said.

"Not as such, no, but I never leave Ellen alone, and the only people I trust to stay with her in my absence are Kathy and Ian. Kathy wasn't available because of that damn charity thing she organised for a local jockey and Wednesday is Ian's skittles night."

"Strange night for a fundraiser," Fiona said.

"You'd have to ask Kathy about that, but the party goers weren't the type of people who have to get up for work on a Thursday morning. Thinking about it, Thursday is a non-hunt day, and I expect she mostly invited hunt members. They're the only wealthy friends she has as far as I'm aware."

"Would Ian have gone to the party after his skittles match?"

"You'd have to ask him, but I doubt it. We're not fancy enough for that bunch of toffs. They accept Kathy because of her horse skills. I understand she's sorted out many an expensive mistake for them. Not that they care about the money. They just want to point score by appearing at the next hunt on a horse that scared the living daylights out of its previous owner."

"Humour me and run through the time Ian came in and went back out again on Wednesday," Peter said.

"As far as I can remember, he came in normal time at about six. Skittles start at seven-thirty, so he went out again straight after he'd showered and eaten."

"Any idea where he was playing?"

Lighting another cigarette, Lucy replied, "You'll have to ask him or his friends."

The conversation faltered and stuttered to a stop as the minutes ticked by. When Lucy looked up and gave him an apologetic smile, Peter asked, "Does your husband regularly go out of an evening without you?"

"A few nights a week he likes to go out for a pint with his mates. They go to The Old Ship mostly as that's still a straight drinking pub."

"Have you ever thought your husband might be having an affair?"

Lucy roared with laughter. "I don't think anyone would be stupid enough. Anyhow, with a community this small I'd soon find out about it. There's probably only a handful of women around here of a similar age, and I somehow can't see a young girl being interested in that grumpy old sod."

"How about someone from out of the area? Like Vivien Morse?"

With a look of amusement at the idea, Lucy drew hard on her cigarette. Through a plume of smoke, she said, "Now you are being ridiculous. Not a chance." After a few minutes of silence, she said, "That's strange. He's normally been and gone by now." Standing, she offered to make fresh coffee which they declined.

"Do you know if your husband heard about Creer's escape this morning?"

Lucy shrugged and flicked on the kettle. "Well, I'm having another. Ian gets up at the crack of dawn, so I never see him first thing. He always has the radio on, though. Says he can't bear the silence anymore, so I expect he has heard by now."

They were interrupted by the sound of Peter's phone ringing. He checked the screen before saying, "Sorry, I need to take this," and walked from the room.

"Does your husband have a phone, Lucy? Could you call him?"

Fiona asked.

Lucy retrieved a phone from a kitchen drawer. After a short while, she said, "Typical. He never answers the damn thing."

"Could you jot the number down and I'll keep trying him." With the number neatly copied into her notepad, Fiona asked, "Do you really think he would have gone after Rob Creer when he heard the news?"

Lucy thought for a while before replying, "I'd say fifty-fifty whether he'd go storming off after him or directly to the nearest off-licence. Either way, he'll be livid and in a blind rage."

Peter re-entered the room. "We're needed back at the station, Mrs Bassett, but it is important we speak to Ian. Could you ask him to contact us as soon as you see him?"

On the way to the car, Fiona asked, "What's the rush?"

"We're heading into Birstall. Jane Salt has been officially reported as missing by her partner."

SIXTEEN

The fog in Rob's head started to clear. He opened his eyes but quickly closed them again, unable to deal with the brightness. His head started to pound, although the grey fuzziness that earlier attached itself to his thoughts didn't return. He slightly opened one eye. To his side was a glass of water and a couple of blister packs of tablets. He had a vague recollection of someone putting them there for him. He popped two tablets from each pack and swallowed them with a gulp of water.

He tried to pull himself fully upright but was overcome by dizziness and nausea. He lay still, keeping his eyes firmly closed, which reduced the pounding headache to a low hum, and started to process the events of the last few hours.

Everything had gone smoothly until Jane had let him out of the car at the edge of some woods in the middle of nowhere. The stupid bitch had failed to tell him the pathway branched in two directions. Sod's Law dictated he had taken the wrong branch and got soaked to the skin in the process as the heavens poured torrential rain down on him. By the time he'd retraced his steps, he'd fallen several times as the rain turned the path into a squelchy, slippery quagmire. He remembered with a shiver how cold, wet and exhausted he'd been when the cottage had come into sight. Recalling the blanket of relief that had settled all around him as he'd stumbled the last few yards towards the cottage door and shelter, he drifted back to sleep.

❖ ❖ ❖

Peter and Fiona were met outside Jane Salt's office by Abbie Ward. Inside Jane's empty office Abbie referred to her notebook. "As you know, yesterday was a scheduled day off and today was booked as a holiday a couple of weeks ago. Jane Salt had arranged to meet a friend near Birmingham, who was moving to a new house following a divorce. The friend, Annette Green, has confirmed she arrived around eight o'clock yesterday and helped her most of the morning. At lunchtime, they went to a local pub for a celebratory drink, and at around three o'clock, Ms Salt left her friend in the pub to drive home. Nobody has seen her since, but her partner thinks she may have returned home for a change of clothes. Her partner was attending a family meal and didn't return home until nearly midnight last night. It had been agreed previously that Ms Salt would meet up with them if she returned home in time and wasn't feeling too tired."

Peter looked out the large window behind the desk that gave a panoramic view of Birstall harbour. More to himself than the others in the room, he said, "So many connections to Birmingham and yet nothing concrete." He spun on his heels. "Where's Litten?"

"Talking to the other employees," Abbie replied. She handed Peter a page ripped from her notebook. "That's the number and address for Sheila Bond, Ms Salt's partner.

She's at the home they shared calling everyone she can think of. Do you want to see her?"

"Once you've finished talking to the employees, I want you and Litten to go back through Vivien Morse's caseload and cross-reference anyone both she and Jane had contact with. Go back as far as you have to until you find someone with grounds to harbour a resentment towards both women. While you're at it, humour me and check the distance from Annette Green's new home to Shoreham Prison. Update me once you have something."

"Will do. Anything else I should be doing?"

Peter hesitated before saying, "I'll let you know if I think of anything."

Returning to the main desk at the entrance to the office complex, Peter asked the receptionist to point him in the direction of the building's security team. With an efficient business-like smile, she replied, "If you take a seat over there, I'll ask Sydney Peck, our head of security, to come down to see you."

Peter made a point of checking his watch but dutifully moved over to the waiting area. They'd hardly taken their seats when they felt the vibrations under their feet from the sprung floor of the approach of a heavily built man. Sydney was instantly recognisable with his sharp crew cut and standard security uniform. He was about six foot, six and almost as wide as he was tall. Beads of sweat ran down his flabby cheeks as he maintained his march towards them. When he thrust out his right hand towards Peter, it was clammy and moist. He announced himself in a deep voice, giving both his name and position as he shook their hands vigorously. On releasing Fiona's hand, he showed them his identity card.

"Is there somewhere nearby we can have a private word?" Peter asked.

"Can I see your identity cards before we proceed?" Sydney said.

While Sydney checked Fiona's warrant card, Peter used the opportunity to wipe his hand on his trouser leg.

"They seem to be all in order. Please follow me."

They were led to a small airless room on the ground floor that had been set up to resemble a police interview room. Taking a seat, Peter said, "Thank you for taking the time to see us. Did you know Vivien Morse and Jane Salt, who worked in this building?"

"Social workers on floor three. Yes, I make it a point to get to know all regular personnel as part of my job." Sydney retrieved a handkerchief from his jacket pocket and mopped his brow, his raised arm wafting the smell of stale sweat around the room. "You said worked. Has Ms Salt been killed like poor Mrs Morse?"

"She's unaccounted for at the moment," Peter replied. "Because of the attack on her employee, we are taking that very seriously.

Have you noticed anyone hanging around the building or acting suspiciously, especially with regards the two women?"

Sydney scratched his head, revealing a dark circle of sweat under the arm of his jacket. "I and my staff take regular walks around the building plus we monitor the cameras covering the main entrance and staff underground car park at all times. Nothing springs to mind. I take special care to see the female workers have left the building safely and I haven't seen anyone who gave me cause for concern."

"If there was an incident within the building, such as a visitor acting aggressively, what would be the procedure?"

"I… I mean security would be called immediately, and we would neutralise the risk of danger. We'd either escort the person out of the building or restrain them until the police arrived, whichever was most appropriate."

Peter pushed the vision of the overweight Sydney sitting on an errant visitor to the building from his mind and asked, "And has that ever happened? Have you or any of your team had to escort anyone from the building?" Sydney shook his head, replying, "No, but it is still early days. The office space has only been rented out the last six months."

"And you and your team haven't had problems with anyone loitering outside?"

"No."

"How long do you keep the tapes from the security cameras?"

"A fortnight and then they're taped over."

Peter stood and pulled a card from his jacket. "Thank you for your time. I'll send an officer to collect the surveillance tapes later today and to take your contact details. We'll be in touch, but if you think of anything relevant in the meantime, please give me a call."

SEVENTEEN

The house shared by Jane Salt and Sheila Bond was an elegant Victorian detached property. It held an imposing, raised position in an upmarket area on the outskirts of Birstall and fronted a large public park. Sheila led them through to a tastefully decorated living room with a double bay window overlooking a surprisingly large rear garden of about a third of an acre. Peter glanced outside before asking, "Are those beehives at the bottom?"

"Yes," Sheila replied, a smile briefly replacing her worried expression. "I like to do my bit for the environment. You should visit in the spring and summer when the flowers are in bloom. Despite being near the centre of town, it's our secret haven of peace and tranquillity. Away from all the hustle and bustle, Jane is a very different person from the career woman everyone sees. I suppose I am as well, if truth be told." Sheila sank into a leather chair by the window and dropped her face into her hands. After giving a heavy sigh, she raised her head. Deep worry lines burrowed into her face although her eyes remained dry. "Of course, you don't care about these things. You must excuse my rambling. I'm not sure of the correct etiquette in this scenario."

Despite Sheila's obvious distress, like her partner Jane Salt, she was impeccably groomed from her perfectly styled hair to her painted toenails. She drew a circle with a forefinger on the arm of the chair. "How do people normally react in this situation?" Peter cleared his throat to speak, but she continued without pausing. "Technically I suppose she's been missing for only a few hours, but it feels like days. Would you be here if it weren't for Vivien Morse? I take it you think the two are connected." Her voice raised in pitch, "Do you think she is dead already?"

Seizing the opportunity to speak, Peter said, "It really is too soon to know anything."

"Will everything have to come out? I mean will it all be in the newspapers and the television?"

The door opened, and a plump, middle-aged woman entered. "Sorry to interrupt, Miss Bond. Can I get anything for you or your guests?"

Sheila jumped from her chair. "How incredibly rude of me. Do accept my apologies. What would you like to drink?"

Peter waved her concern aside. "I'm good."

"I'm fine, thank you," Fiona said.

"We seem to be fine, Jean. Your money is in the usual place. I'll see you tomorrow," Sheila said.

Jean hovered in the entrance to the room. "Would you like me to stay longer, Miss Bond? It's really no problem. You shouldn't be alone at a time like this."

"That's so terribly sweet of you to ask, but I'm okay. You go on home. My brother is on his way."

Jean gave the three of them a curt nod and withdrew from the room. Once the door closed, Sheila gave a sharp intake of breath. "Where do we go from here?"

"The better the picture we can create of Jane's interests and movements over the past few weeks, the more likely we are to discover what has happened or where she may be," Fiona replied.

Over the following hour, which was interrupted several times by concerned friends calling, Sheila painted a picture of a devoted couple who had been together for ten years living a quiet if privileged lifestyle without enemies. Sheila gave the impression she was very much in love, if not besotted, with Jane, causing Fiona to jot in her notepad, 'Check with friends how perfect the relationship really is.'

Once they had all they needed, including a clear photograph of

Jane, Peter said, "Before we go would you mind telling me what you do for a living?"

"Of course. I'm a barrister working out of Halls in London."

"That's a long commute for you each day."

"Not really. Less than two hours by train. Our privacy is very important. To both of us," Sheila said.

The room, along with the house's location, screamed affluence. Peter judged some of the original signed artwork on the walls probably cost more than his car. "You have a lovely house, but I wouldn't want your mortgage payments."

"Oh, Daddy bought the house for me when I attended university here. I loved the area so much I stayed."

Peter leaned forward in his chair. "Are your parents and work colleagues aware of your sexuality?"

Sheila stared back with narrowed eyes. "The subject has never come up, and as I said, we value our privacy. Do you tell your colleagues, 'by the way I'm heterosexual, and I sometimes have sex with my wife?' Well?" She studied Peter's reaction for a short while before adding, "I thought not. So why should I?"

Ignoring the challenge in Sheila's tone and meeting her defiant stare, Peter asked, "Have you ever been threatened or blackmailed with regards your relationship with Jane Salt?"

The room filled with silent anticipation until Sheila finally said, "No. That has never happened."

Accepting the poker face was not going to falter, Peter stood. "Thank you, Miss Bond. We'll be in contact. Should you hear anything or think of something that might help us locate Miss Salt, please contact us immediately."

"Yes, of course."

"One other thing. Have you suffered a break-in recently?"

"Not exactly. A few weeks back I had this strange sensation someone had been in the house. I couldn't work out what it was, but something seemed out of place. Nothing was taken as far as I could see, and Jane told me I was being silly. Maybe I was, but I still felt violated in some hidden way. Does that make any sense?"

Peter gave a sympathetic nod before asking, "But nothing was taken?"

"Nothing of mine and Jane insisted nothing of hers was taken but… This sounds stupid, although Jane insisted I was imagining things, she seemed more upset and jumpy afterwards."

"This may sound an equally strange question, but did you notice any dog hairs in the house afterwards?" Peter said.

"Yes, yes I did. Jane said I was overreacting. She pointed out that Jean my housekeeper, has a dog and the hairs were probably carried in her clothes. Or maybe she brings her dog to work with her if she thinks neither of us will be here."

They were about to leave when Fiona said, "Sheila Bond! Sorry I've just remembered where I've seen your name recently. You were the junior barrister on Rob Creer's defence team."

"That's correct. It was the first high profile case I handled. Why? Is it somehow relevant to Jane going missing?"

"I don't know. You tell me," Peter said re-taking his seat. "Would Jane have come into contact with your client?"

Sheila's brow creased in concentration. "I'm trying to think. It was a long time ago, and of course, he's still in prison."

"Was. He escaped yesterday," Peter said.

Sheila's hand shot to her mouth. "And you think this is connected to Jane's disappearance? I can't see how that could be, or what possible interest he'd have in her. I don't think they ever met. I remember she came to watch a couple of the days of the trial." Sheila tapped the side of her head as if chiding herself for her poor memory. "I do remember something now. Jane said Creer started to stare at her as if he knew she was my partner. Oh God! Do you think he's taken her to punish me for not getting him off? I was only the junior on the case, but I did have the most direct contact with him."

"What did you think of him? Is he the type to go looking for revenge?"

"Without a doubt. He had a massive chip on his shoulder. Initially, he was all sickly charm with me. Once he realised I wasn't going to be interested in him, the façade dropped instantly.

Underneath was a spoilt little boy who thought the whole world was picking on him for no good reason. He then tried to use his childhood to gain sympathy. The psychiatrist we instructed advised against using the details because of the privileged life he walked into. As I remember, Barbara, that's the psychiatrist we used, was quite convinced he was of sound mind and there was no chance of suggesting diminished responsibility."

Sheila moved to a bureau in the corner of the room. "I'm still in contact with Barbara. She lives and practices in central London. I have her contact details here somewhere," she said, riffling through the drawers. "We still instruct her as an expert witness for important cases, although these days her rates are astronomical. Here we are." Sheila handed a cream business card to Fiona and sat back down.

"What was the childhood issue?" Fiona asked.

"He was left on the steps of a church in Manchester when he was only a few hours old. I believe it had a great deal of media attention at the time. He was very fortunate to be adopted by an extremely wealthy couple. Professional people. A banker and a doctor I think, but you'd have to check that. Creer received a top class private education and anything else his heart desired from fast cars to polo ponies. There was absolutely no need for him to turn to a life of crime."

"I don't remember that coming out at the time of the trial," Peter said.

"We didn't feel it would help his case. Surprisingly the media didn't pick up on it. As well as standard rejection issues Barbara looked into the nature/nurture angle. Neither argument was put forward at the trial in the end. But none of it was my decision. I was little more than Bentley's gofer at the time."

"Bentley?"

"Sir Bentley. Leading barrister in the case. He died of cancer a few months ago. I attended his funeral."

Peter stood to leave. "Thank you for your time, Ms Bond. Would you mind if we took a quick look in Jane's bedroom before we leave?"

"Our bedroom," Sheila replied. After another deep sigh, she said, "Go ahead. We've nothing to hide."

Peter telephoned Abbie Ward on route to the car. "Are you and Litten still questioning the other employees? ...Good. Have you checked whether any of them have been broken into at home recently? If they have, and I appreciate this sounds odd, but ask them if they found dog hairs afterwards. Also, find out if any of them have had problems with anyone hanging around the area or sensed they were being watched or followed when they left the building. Any complaints at all are relevant. One last thing. Before you leave, could you collect the security tapes from the head of security and take a statement from him? Okay. See you back at the station later."

Fiona asked, "Do you think both incidents are work-related, and someone did break into their homes looking for some sort of document?"

"Possibly. More likely than the hypothetical theory that Creer is on the hunt for revenge, anyway. The dog hairs suggest the same person was responsible for the two break-ins and he was in prison then. He was also under supervision in a hospital bed when Vivien was attacked."

"He has a solid alibi, but he could have someone doing his dirty work. According to Dick, his escape had been planned for a while," Fiona said.

"I do wish we didn't have that idiot Dick muddying the waters. I'm convinced the reason he's in the area is somehow connected to Creer. I've yet to meet a normal burglar who takes his dog along to break-ins. He takes that dog with him everywhere and hardly comes close to the definition of normal. The only thing I know for sure about him is that he is lying to us."

"Dick carried on drinking in the pub after Vivien stormed out and wasn't seen making any contact with Jane," Fiona pointed out. "The landlord was pretty adamant he was too drunk to do anything other than collapse into bed and sleep it off. Other than the stabbing he was falsely arrested for, there is nothing in his background to suggest a violent nature."

"Don't forget at the present time, Jane is only missing. She might turn up out of the blue embarrassed by all the fuss."

"Really?"

"Unlikely, I admit, but not impossible," Peter said.

"I've just remembered something Gladys told me in the pub when you were buying the drinks. Before he found Druidism, Dick was a solicitor. There's the possibility he knew Sheila Bond previously in a professional capacity."

"Interesting. That needs looking into. As the two women didn't socialise out of work, didn't share any interests or hobbies or even taste in type of partners, the link seems to be work-related rather than a personal matter," Peter said.

"I have thought of yet another possibility other than the tenuous link to Creer. What if Vivien was an unfortunate case of mistaken identity?"

"In what way?" Peter asked.

"Bear with me. I'm thinking out loud here," Fiona said. "The break-ins could be very relevant. Somebody looking for something work-related? Only Jane Salt would have greater overall access to anything sensitive. It could even be something more personal. Sheila Bond is clearly very wealthy, well-connected and with a high-profile career. She clearly hides her sexuality, so Jane Salt could be a kidnap situation. Only initially they grabbed the wrong woman and killed her once they'd realised their mistake?"

"A possibility, I guess," Peter said.

"Is Sheila Bond likely to contact us if she receives a blackmail request?"

"My first thought is she'd try to pay herself out of the situation. It might be worth looking at Bond's recent court cases and see if anything leaps out."

"Meanwhile, what should we do about Dick? He's still being held," Fiona reminded him.

"Once the search of his van is complete, I'm going to have another go at trying to persuade him to say what he's really doing here and question him about the two break-ins. Just mentioning the dog hairs may get him to start talking if he thinks we could match them to his dog."

"And Ian Bassett? Should I carry on trying to get hold of him?" Fiona asked.

"Definitely. He remains a person of interest until we have a clearer idea of what's going on here. I'm afraid it's going to be a laborious process going through a lot of files looking for connections. Interviewing Bassett will be a welcome break from the station-based research when he turns up."

EIGHTEEN

Robbie opened his eyes and stretched out in the bed. He felt fully rested but hungry. He sat bolt upright. The last thing he remembered was falling asleep in a rocking chair nursing a bottle of whisky. He lifted the duvet to check. How did he end up naked in bed and what had stained his hand? He cupped his hands around his nose. They smelt coppery. He continued looking at his hands, turning them over. It looked like dried blood. The same stain marked his chest.

He collected his clothes which were strewn across the bare floorboards. His feet curled up on the cold surface as he inspected his clothing. There were a few reddish, brown splatters on his jeans, but his sweatshirt was stiff and stuck together in places by semi-dried blood. What the hell happened? He checked himself over. He had a few scratches on his forearms but nothing to explain the amount of blood on his clothing. He staggered to the mirror, hanging on to the wall to steady himself. His legs felt rubbery, and he didn't trust their ability to hold his weight. The mirror revealed he had a couple of red scratch marks on one cheek.

He crossed the room and sat heavily on the side of the bed. Gingerly touching the side of his face, he convinced himself the marks were from stray brambles. Spotting a black canvas holdall tucked neatly against the wall at the head of the bed, he tentatively pulled it towards himself and unzipped it. Inside were several changes of clothes all recently purchased, a hair dyeing product, a pay as you go mobile phone and a bundle of cash. Everything he'd asked Jane to provide. Yet he had no recollection of seeing her since she'd dropped him off at the edge of the woods.

Selecting a fresh set of clothes and laying them out on the bed, he reasoned Jane must have left the bag in the room much earlier. He just hadn't seen it when he'd put himself to bed. Hell, he didn't even remember going to bed, so it was hardly likely he would have noticed the black bag in the dark. A good long shower and a mug of strong coffee and he'd be as right as rain.

Carrying the clothes under his arm, he pulled back the curtains at the window. Outside was grey and dreary but at least it wasn't raining. A typical autumn day in good old merry England. He couldn't wait to collect his money and escape the damp dull place. Soon he'd be browning himself under a warm Mediterranean sun.

He stopped abruptly in the corridor. There were blood splatters on the floor, and blood smears up the wall. He followed the patterns to an interior door. Taking a deep breath, he grabbed the handle and turned it. Inside was a bright sunny kitchen painted yellow and full of sparkly white appliances. The centrepiece was the bloodied corpse of Jane Salt sprawled across the black and white floor tiles.

Rob tiptoed around her, analysing the frenzied stab marks from every angle. The slash wound across her throat was so deep she had almost been decapitated.

He bent over the corpse and pulled the carving knife from between her shoulder blades. He rinsed it under the tap before using it to cut a couple of slices of bread from the loaf on the side. He popped them in the toaster while he made some coffee. Sitting at the small table eating his breakfast, he raised his mug in a toast to his faithful lover, "To Jane."

Although he had planned on killing her eventually, it was an experience he had wanted to remember. It was always a little galling when things happened during his episodes, and he felt robbed of the memory. He took his time enjoying the thrill of eating breakfast naked. He studied with interest how the cold raised the hairs on his arms before heading to the shower with the hair dye.

By the time darkness started to fall, Rob was in an agitated state. The lack of conversation from Jane had annoyed him, and he'd returned to the rocking chair with the bottle of whisky. With only half the contents left, he'd rationed himself. He'd dozed for a few hours after the strain of trying to recollect what had happened to Jane. A vague recollection of a stag had come to him but no other details.

He paced the room, stopping only to pull the curtain aside to check the remaining light. He could still see the outline of the trees in the distance as the wind buffeted them, making them look like dancing skeletons. He pressed his forehead against the cold of the window pane. He crossed his fingers, hoping he'd find Ellen, recover the cash and be on his way out of the country to a new life as Tom Hutton with his little woman by his side by the early hours of tomorrow.

Finally, he could no longer make out the outline of the old oak tree at the bottom of the garden. He checked himself in the mirror. Pleased with his new appearance, he was looking forward to discovering whether blondes really do have more fun. He clicked his flashlight on and off and ran his eyes over the directions to Park Farm one last time. He wrapped himself in the old Barbour coat he'd found hanging in one of the wardrobes and headed out the door.

He wrinkled his nose in disgust as the musty smell from the coat mingled with the damp smell of wet grass and sodden earth. At least he looked the part of a bumbling village idiot, and it kept out the cold wind that whistled through the trees. The last of the autumn leaves fluttered around him as they fell to the wet mulch. The way the soaked bedraggled leaves muffled the sound of his steps he took to be a sign that things were going to go his way.

Initially, he thought his mind was playing tricks on him when he heard the occasional, faint sounds of singing. The deeper into the woods he walked, the more the notes joined together and became louder. Only it wasn't the sweet song of a forest nymph he'd first imagined. It was more of an out-of-tune wailing accompanied by heavy thuds of clumsy movement.

A mangy dog appeared, barking angrily at him. He forced himself through a clump of bramble to hide, receiving stinging scratches to his hands and face and tried to shoo the dog away. With a snort of contempt, the dog relieved itself on the straggly bush and trotted away. Rob's eyes adjusted to the dark as he watched the dog's exit. Or maybe it was because his eyes widened in surprise when he caught sight of the dog's owner and that allowed more light to hit the back of his retinas.

He crouched down lower, peering through a small gap in the brambles, mesmerised by the bizarre display in the small clearing. "What the hell?" he muttered under his breath.

NINETEEN

A chubby middle-aged woman wearing a flowing white negligee and a garland of twigs precariously perched upon her head pranced around in wild circles. She threw petals into the air while chanting some random nonsense. Spinning around on the spot, she raised her arms towards the sky before flopping to the ground in a panting heap. Rob was about to creep away when the crazed woman pulled her considerable weight onto her knees and bent forwards. She thumped the wet grass with the palms of her hands, shrieking, "Release my Dick!"

Rob could contain his laughter no longer. Covering his mouth with a hand to muffle the sound, he stumbled backwards, slipping on the wet ground. His damaged leg gave way, and he fell, landing flat on his back. The dog reappeared, growling and barking at the bush he'd been hiding behind.

"Dick? Dick? Is that you my love?"

Rob looked up into the snarling teeth of the dog inches from his face as its heavy front paws pressed heavily on his chest. He recoiled, feeling sick as slobber from the dog's jaws landed in his eyes. Wiping the blob seemed to merely smear it around his face, so he tried to flick the sticky substance from the side of his face only to find it stuck to his fingers. Wiping his hand on the wet grass, he tried and failed to arch his back to push the dog away. The dog pressed down harder on his chest as a huge string of slobber swayed like a pendulum from its mouth. As it stretched closer to his face, he could stand it no longer and shouted, "Call off your bloody dog!"

"Colin, darling. Leave the nasty man alone and come here."

With a final show of teeth and a low growl depositing the long strand of drool on Rob's face, the dog withdrew to its mistress. Rob scrambled to his feet, his previous good humour turning quickly to anger. Exiting from behind the brambles, he came nose to nose with a pink round face and accusing hazel eyes.

Pulling a brown leaf from a mass of unruly hair, Gladys said, "How dare you spy on me! Can a woman not have her privacy?"

Straightening his wet and muddy clothes, Rob shouted, "Madam. I was certainly not spying on you while you... What exactly were you doing?"

"Not that it is any concern of yours, I was asking the trees to release my Dick."

Rob took a step backwards with a furtive look upwards at the treetops. It wasn't often he was lost for words, especially in the company of women. Usually, he could charm his way out of any situation but there was crazy, and there was stark crazy bonkers. Normal crazy he could deal with, but this was definitely the latter.

"I might ask you the same question. What exactly are you doing creeping about the woods at this time of the night?" Gladys asked. "And who are you anyway? I don't recognise you as someone from around here."

Unwilling to answer the question and playing for time, Rob gave her his best cheeky grin. "Only might?" Looking around for a stick or a stone on the ground, he stuck out his hand and said, "We seem to have gotten off to a bad start." Racking his brains to think of something to say before she realised who he was and set the dog on him again, he added, "My name is Bob and ..."

Before he could say anything more, he was engulfed in a florally scented bear hug. "Oh, thank you, trees, for sending my Dick's friend Bob to help me in my hour of need."

Gladys dragged him to a fallen tree and sat him down. She produced a bottle of whisky and a glass from behind the log. "Dick has told me all about you. How you stood by him when he was wrongly accused of murdering your poor wife. You must think me quite bananas. I wasn't convinced all this chanting malarkey that Dick believes in would actually work. But darling, you know how it is. I was sat at home all by my lonesome and thought I might as well give it a go. I couldn't sleep anyway, and I always say, nothing ventured, nothing gained."

Rob nodded and offered the glass he'd filled to Gladys.

"Not for me, sweetie. I'm already a little tipsy. Now, darling, you must tell me everything you know and how you found out so quickly."

Reaching behind the log for a broken branch to use as a club while taking a sip of whiskey, Rob replied, "Maybe it would be quicker if you filled me in on the details."

"Of course, pumpkin," Gladys replied, grasping his forearm before he could close his fingers around the branch. "Simply because my gentle Dick is a practising Druid, has been in prison and only recently arrived in the area, the police have accused him of the murder of a woman found in the woods near here. They burst into my home without warning in a most alarming manner and stole my poor Dick away. The cruel and heartless police are keeping that dear gentle soul, we both love dearly, in custody."

Twigging Dick was the pompous idiot from prison, Rob freed his hand to stroke his chin, pretending to be in deep thought. "But he was falsely imprisoned for the stabbing of my dear wife. They released him when they realised they'd made a mistake."

"Yes, darling, and you, of course, know all about what really happened. Tomorrow morning, we can go to the station together, and you can explain all of that, and then they'll have to release him. Oh! How could they make the same dreadful assumption twice?" Wringing her hands, she added, "It's so beastly unfair."

"Who knows how their minds work but of course I will visit the station with you. Anything to help my old friend." Rob knocked back the rest of the whisky. "It does seem the police were very quick to jump to their conclusions. Did they give any additional explanation, or did they simply grab him without one?"

"Maybe I will have some of that," Gladys said, reaching for the empty glass. Placing it between her knees, she poured in a generous measure. "It's all quite confusing and frightening. They did say something about it being for his own safety. Then, they returned and took his van away."

"How curious," Rob said, taking the bottle from her and screwing the lid back on. "What do you suppose they meant by his own safety?"

"I think it was something to do with a prison escape. They asked him a lot of questions about a man called Rob Creer."

"Did they?" Rob asked, taking the glass from Gladys and gulping down most of the contents. "What did he say about this Creer fellow?"

Gladys gave a girlish giggle. "Oh, you naughty thing making his name sound like he's a queer. How frightfully funny. Dick will love that when I tell him."

"Let's be serious a moment, my dear," Rob said, handing the glass back to her and dropping his hand behind the log. "I'm very keen to help out my old friend as quickly as possible. To do that I need to know how his connection to this other inmate fits into his arrest and why he should need protection from him."

"Do you know, my dear, I have absolutely no idea," Gladys replied, reaching for his hand again. "First thing in the morning we can sort it all out with those silly policemen."

Freeing his hand, Rob gave Gladys a quick pat on her knee before casually letting it drop behind him. "Well, what did Dick tell you about this Creer man?"

"Just that he's a vile, odious little man." Gladys pulled him closer by his shoulder just as he got a firm hold on the length of wood. Giggling she whispered, "Dick spotted him in the showers once and noticed he had an incredibly small you know what," pointing to his groin. "Dick thinks it's his smallness in that area that made him such a horrible bully."

"Really?" Rob said, with a wide smile as he swung the branch down on her head. There was a satisfying crack as Gladys crumpled into a heap at his feet. He lifted the stick over his shoulder, preparing to give a fatal blow, when the dog leapt at him, sinking its teeth into the elbow of his jacket. Regaining his balance, Rob changed the stick into his other hand and whacked the dog across its back. It released its hold on his jacket and fell whimpering to the ground. Rob kicked it hard in the side while raising the stick in the air for a second swipe. Before he could take aim, the dog was scarpering away through the trees.

He turned his attention back to Gladys still motionless in a heap on the ground. He took aim when a thought occurred to him. If the police were already onto him, they might be watching Ellen. Damn. If he couldn't recover the money tonight, a dead body so close to the cottage would lead them straight to him. If only Ellen's father hadn't turned Jane away, he'd already have the key and only have to locate the safe. Maybe he should concentrate on recovering the safe and worry about how to force it open later.

He sat on the log and poured himself a fresh whisky. He was deep in thought when he heard Gladys groan and try to roll herself over. He threw the glass down and grabbed hold of Gladys' arm and roughly pulled her to her feet. She swayed side to side with a glazed look on her face.

"Come on," he said, pulling her in the direction of the cottage. She stumbled and fell onto one knee. He hauled her back to her feet. "Walk, God, damn it."

Gladys tottered sideways before righting herself and putting her hand to her forehead. "Where are we going, darling? I feel quite strange. Did I have too much juice?"

"Something like that," Rob said, steadying her by her elbow. "Walk with me to my cottage. It's not far, and we can get you all sorted out there."

Gladys chuckled and nearly took another tumble. "You're not the big bad wolf, are you? You're not taking me to your secret hideaway to have your wicked way with me, are you?"

"Highly unlikely," Rob muttered.

"What was that, you naughty boy?"

Rob moved behind Gladys and holding her right shoulder with one arm and her left elbow with the other, he roughly propelled her along the track to the cottage. He really didn't care anymore what she thought. Sooner or later she'd be dead. And if she didn't shut up it, would be far sooner.

He was bathed in sweat despite the cool night air by the time he propped her against the side of the door while he searched his pockets for the house keys. Once he unlocked the door, she fell forwards into the hallway, nearly taking him with her. Her legs were buckling underneath her by the time he heaved her along the corridor and pushed her into the spare bedroom. Once he let go, she stumbled a few steps and collapsed face down onto the narrow, unmade bed.

TWENTY

"Peter!" Fiona called across the room. "We might have something here. We have a possible witness. Mrs Abigail Tuck is positive she saw Jane Salt arguing in the lane with Ian Bassett the evening she went missing."

Peter took a sip from his first coffee of the morning before replying, "Whereabouts and what time?"

"Right outside Bassett's farmhouse. Mrs Tuck's daughter had gone to play at a school friend's house, and she was on her way to collect her. She thinks it was a little after four o'clock."

Peter groaned. "The time doesn't work. She'd still have been on the M5. Her friend Annette said Jane didn't leave the pub until around three."

"Ah," Fiona said, her face full of disappointment. "Sorry, you're right. I should have realised."

Peter got up from his chair and stretched. "Have you got an address? I think it still might be worth having a word with her. She could have been wrong about the time."

"Yes. It's only a few miles from Park farm."

"By the way, did Ian Bassett ever get back to you?" Peter asked.

"No, he didn't. I'll try him again now."

"Get hold of this Abigail Tuck first. We'll visit Ian Bassett straight after."

Abigail Tuck was an attractive young mother of three children, all under the age of eight years old, who proved herself to be a credible witness. She was adamant she saw Ian and Jane arguing quite forcibly in the lane outside Park Farm no later than shortly after four o'clock. Her memory of the event was crystal clear. She had telephoned ahead because she was running late to collect her daughter at four, so was annoyed to see two people blocking the narrow lane. A car she assumed belonged to Jane was parked close to the hedgerow, but the driver's door was wide open. The pair of them stood in the middle of the lane arguing, oblivious to what was going on around them. Abigail had to stop and beep her horn before they finally moved to the side of the lane to let her pass. She made a point of glaring angrily at them for their delay in moving out of her path.

It was only after settling the three children in a separate room to watch a cartoon that Abigail collected her diary from a side drawer and showed them the entry in her neat handwriting. It was four o'clock she was supposed to be collecting her daughter, but Abigail was talking about the previous week.

During the short drive from Abigail Tuck's home to Park Farm, Fiona telephoned Shoreham Prison. She completed the call as Peter parked in front of the farmhouse.

"There have been no sightings of Rob Creer to date, but they've confirmed he had a string of regular female visitors and he exchanged letters with many more. One of his regulars visited every other Friday and was called Claire Biro, but they have no records of Vivien or Jane visiting him."

Peter pulled the car key out of the ignition. "Interesting. Friday happens to be Jane Salt's regular day off. I don't suppose visitors would have to give their real names. The second we've finished here, get her photograph sent up there and ask for an urgent reply as to whether she was his regular Friday visitor."

"Will do. Poor Sheila. She was under the impression Jane was visiting her elderly mother in a nursing home every Friday."

Making his way to the front door, Peter said, "She still might have been."

Lucy Bassett opened her front door with the customary cigarette in her hand. She flicked the ash from the end out of the door before saying, "What's he done?"

"What do you mean by that?" Peter asked.

"Ian. That's what you're here for, isn't it? I take it he has gone and got himself in some type of bother up north. I told him to come home and leave it to the police to sort out. But as usual, one word from me and he totally ignores it. So, come on. What has he done?"

"We haven't heard anything. We were hoping to be able to speak to him here," Peter said.

"When did you speak to him?" Fiona asked. "I've been trying to get hold of him ever since our last visit."

Lucy flicked her cigarette out the door and folded her arms across her chest. "And I told him to contact you. I can't help it if he chose not to, can I?"

"When was this?" Peter asked.

"Just after you left the last time. He rang to say he was on his way up to Birmingham to find Rob Creer. I told him to stop being such a daft bugger and come home. I haven't heard from him since. If you don't know where he is, then he could be anywhere."

"Could we come in a minute?" Peter asked.

Lucy stepped back to let them pass. "Be my guest, but you won't find him here. I'm not a liar like some people around here."

Once settled in the kitchen, Peter asked, "Do you know Abigail Tuck?"

"That snooty woman from up the road? Yes, I do. Thinks a lot of herself, that one, just because her husband has some top-notch job in London. Probably has a little bit on the side up there and all. Serve her right if he does."

"Do you know Jane Salt?" Peter asked.

Lucy looked confused. "Name rings a bell, but I can't place her. Nope, sorry."

"You might have seen the name recently in the newspapers or on the local news. She's the woman who has gone missing recently, and Abigail Tuck saw her arguing with your husband outside here just over a week ago."

Enlightenment filled Lucy's eyes, and she reached for a fresh cigarette. "Oh her. Yeah, I thought that was strange. I assumed the paper had made a mistake."

"A mistake? How come?" Fiona asked.

"The papers said she was a social worker like Vivian. But she was a journalist wanting to do a piece on our poor Ellen. Yeah, I remember her. Our Ian sent her packing with her tail between her legs."

"A journalist? You're quite sure about that?"

Exhaling a long trail of smoke, Lucy replied, "That's what she told Ian she was."

"Had you ever seen the woman before?"

"No. Ian told me about her and what happened. I'm not surprised he reacted the way he did. We had a gut-full of journalists up north. He said it was because she wanted to interview Ellen alone in her place. He didn't want Ellen upset by it all being raked up again, but I reckon it was because he got the sense she was sympathetic to Creer. Wanted to get him an early release or something like that."

"You didn't actually see the woman?" Peter asked.

Stubbing her cigarette in the ashtray, Lucy replied, "Oh, but I did, if only from the bedroom window. I heard voices and looked out. It was starting to get dark after such a miserable day weather-wise, but her car headlights were on. I still couldn't see everything that well except her face as she turned towards her car to leave. I could tell it was Ian from his voice and then when he came back to the house, he was right wound up. Come to think of it, I'm not positive he would have mentioned it if I hadn't asked what all the ruckus was about. I can tell you when he came inside he had a face like thunder. He looked fit to explode, so I didn't ask too many questions."

"And you're absolutely sure the woman you saw arguing with your husband was the woman the media are calling Jane Salt?" Peter said.

"The one on the news last night reported as missing? Yes, I'm sure."

"I'm sorry to have to say this, but I'm going to arrange a full search of this house and the rooms along the way where Ellen lives," Peter said.

"You'll be wasting your time, then, as well as causing my daughter a lot of unnecessary upset. I can tell you my Ian has a temper, especially when he has had a drink, but he would never harm a woman. I can categorically state that woman got in her car and left here fit and well. Whatever has happened to her since has nothing to do with us. All of Ian's anger and bitterness is directed at that brute Creer, who ruined our Ellen's life."

Peter raised an eyebrow, "And possibly someone sympathetic to him?"

Lucy propelled herself away from the table and stood with her arms firmly folded across her chest. "You're barking up the wrong tree here. You should be trying to recapture the bastard, not harassing his innocent victims. I dread to think how Ellen will react to having strangers going through her private things. I'm not sure I'll be able to manage her on my own. If she ends up back in that hospital, I'll hold you personally responsible. Heaven only knows what Ian will say when he hears about it."

"Well maybe if he contacts us he could have some say in the matter," Peter said. He softened his voice and added, "Would it help if Fiona and another woman officer stayed with you both during the search?"

Lucy sucked hard on yet another cigarette. "You mean pin her to the floor while I call the men in white coats to come and collect her?"

"Is she really likely to react that badly?" Fiona asked. When Lucy nodded her head, Fiona caught Peter's eye and said, "Maybe we could give you time to contact your doctor to see if he'll prescribe something to help keep her calm during the search?"

Peter looked at Lucy, "I'm happy to wait if you'd like to call your doctor now. We can also arrange for some place where you can stay out of the way while they're here."

"I'll call the doctor, but we won't be taking you up on the offer of somewhere to stay. We'll make our own arrangements, if you don't mind."

TWENTY-ONE

Peter paced the floor at the station waiting for word from Fiona who was out at Park Farm with Abbie Ward. Shoreham Prison had positively identified Jane Salt as Rob Creer's regular visitor. A picture of Ian Bassett had been circulated around Birmingham stations, but he'd heard nothing back so far.

He picked up the photograph of Rob Creer for the tenth time, wondering just what the women saw in him. To his way of thinking, Creer's dark hair and tanned hard features made him look dirty and grubby rather than attractive. Only his oddly piercing pale blue eyes stood out as anything remarkable. He was relatively short, only five foot, eight inches according to his records and was of a slight, wiry build. Hardly a hunk.

"Sir?" DC Humphries interrupted Peter's thoughts. "Dick Dee-ath is downstairs. Says he only wants to speak to you."

Peter slipped the photograph of Creer back into the file. "I wonder what the lying toad wants now. The only reason he's not still in custody is nothing incriminating was found in his van, and nobody bothered to collect a sample of the dog hairs found in Vivien's house after the break-in. They have released his van back to him, haven't they?"

"Yes. Minus the small stash of weed they found."

"Okay. I'll go and find out what he wants, but if anything is heard from Ian Bassett, or from the farm search, please let me know at once. And his name is Death, not Dee-ath."

Peter was hardly through the door into the waiting area when

Dick came up close, too close, invading his personal space.

"He's taken her," Dick announced dramatically.

Squeezing through the half-open door, Peter said, "Taken who?"

"Gladys! Rob Creer has taken my Gladys!"

Wondering when she became his Gladys, Peter wearily turned to Sykes, the desk sergeant, and asked, "Which interview rooms are vacant?"

Sykes looked sternly over the top of his half-moon glasses and replied, "They're all currently available, but I can't allow that dog through there."

Colin, the dog, pushed her body against Dick's leg, and it was clear from Dick's face he was not prepared to leave the dog behind.

"We'll talk in the coffee shop," Peter said.

"If you are referring to the establishment in the high street, they do not welcome our canine friends either and Colin is central to my concerns. I believe she has already suffered great trauma, so I cannot consent to another parting." Dick's face brightened. "The Squire Inn at the top of the high street, however, is most accommodating."

"Lead the way," Peter replied.

Once he'd bought a half pint of Bishop's Finger for himself and a ridiculously expensive flute of champagne for Dick, Peter settled them in an alcove in the corner of the bar. "What's this all about, Dick?"

Dick stamped the stone floor with his staff. "Gladys. He's taken Gladys. I know he has."

Peter placed the pad he'd brought with him on the table and reached for the staff. "Put that down or give it to me," he ordered. Satisfied the staff had been put out of reach, he interlaced his fingers and stretched out his arms. "Start at the beginning and explain why you think he's taken her."

"She's not at home," Dick replied, as if this was all that was required for a full nationwide search to be launched immediately.

"I'm afraid I'll need more than that. What time did you realise she was not at home?"

"By the time you good fellows had completed all your procedures, it was late morning when I took my first glorious breath of freedom. I waited another hour for my Bertha to be returned to me. I drove immediately to find Gladys to no avail. Her property was devoid of her wonderful aura. I sensed this loss before alighting from my trusted chariot."

Doodling on the corner of the pad, Peter asked, "What time did you arrive at the house?"

"By the position of the sun, midday had passed."

"And by your watch?" Peter said, pointedly looking at the gold watch on Dick's wrist.

After a sip of champagne, Dick confirmed, "Two o'clock."

Peter raised his eyes to the ceiling. Trying to keep annoyance from his voice, he said, "Over two hours after opening time. Have you checked all the pubs in the area?"

"No. She said she would wait forever for me to return to her."

Throwing the pen onto the pad Peter said, "Maybe so, but I doubt that extended to waiting at home if the pubs were open."

"My good man, you are speaking yet again out of turn and without full knowledge of the circumstances that greeted me on arrival. On my approach to my beloved's abode, I was immediately alerted to things being quite amiss. This was even before I took one step onto the property."

Picking up the pen Peter said, "The house was broken into? Why on earth didn't you say that earlier? Were there signs of a struggle or a note?"

Dick closed his eyes and raised his right hand to stop Peter carrying on. "The house was adequately secured and unviolated."

Peter gave a sigh of relief and took a drink from his dimpled mug of beer. "I think you should wait at the house for Gladys to return, but if you're really worried about her, ring round the local pubs. I suggest you start with The Horseshoe Inn. In the unlikely event, none of the bar staff have seen her today, go and check whether her horse is in its field. She may very well be out horse riding."

Before Peter could stop him, Dick grabbed up his staff and banged it loudly on the floor. This gave the nearby customers an excuse to stare directly at him rather than limiting themselves to giving him furtive glances. "But what about Colin?"

"Take her with you."

"No. No. No," Dick replied, slapping his massive palms on the table top, the impacts causing a mini tsunami in Peter's mug. "When I arrived at the property, poor Colin was whimpering at the front door. Gladys would never be so heartless to lock her outside and go off and leave her. She must have been forced against her will. It is the only obvious explanation."

"Really?" Peter asked sarcastically, with a pained look on his face. "I can think of several others. Maybe she took Colin with her, but something startled the dog and it ran home?"

"Now we're making progress," Dick said, handing the champagne flute to Peter. "Replenish your amber liquid, and we'll elaborate on what could have been so startling my valiant Colin would leave Gladys' side when I'd given firm instructions to guard her."

Peter placed the glass in the centre of the table and remained sitting. "Here's the deal. You promise to tell me why you are here, what it is you've been looking for in the woods and the exact nature of the connection between yourself and Rob Creer. In return, I will get you another drink and discuss what may have happened to Gladys. If you're not going to help me, then I'm afraid I can't help you."

Dick closed his eyes and put his fingertips to his temples.

"Well?" Peter said.

"For Gladys, I will reveal my secrets to you."

Placing a fresh round of drinks on the table, Peter said, "No more messing about. Why are you here and what have you been looking for?"

"But what about Gladys? This isn't going to help us rescue her."

Peter quickly snatched the flute of champagne from the table top and held it over a plant pot on the window sill. "I'd be just as happy to pour this in here. Tell me the truth about your relationship with Rob Creer, and then I'll consider how likely it is that Gladys is in need of rescuing from him."

"I have told you the truth…" Dick stopped talking as Peter tilted the glass over the plant pot. "You have to believe me when I say we are not that kind of friends or working together." Dick's eyes widened as Peter tilted the glass a little more. "But you are correct. I came down here because of Rob Creer. He'd boasted so many times about his money being safely hidden and the beautiful lady that waited for him here I wanted to see if I could find it myself. Not for my benefit, of course. I planned to hand over whatever I discovered to the police. I regret to admit my motivation for this endeavour was pure revenge. I wished to punish Creer for all the humiliation he forced me to endure."

Dick shook his head furiously. "It was absolutely not to make any gain for myself." He reached across the table for the champagne flute. "I'd do anything to see the look on his face when he realised his fortune had been taken from him. Knowing it was returned to its rightful owners would be sufficient gratification for me. Financial rewards mean so very little."

"Although they do help with the expense of champagne." Peter placed the glass on the centre of the table and pushed it towards Dick. "Did you meet Vivien Morse in the woods? Was she the beautiful lady and did she remain loyal to Creer until the end?"

Dick shook his head. "I had nothing to do with the attack on that poor woman. One thing I can tell you is that she was not the one Creer entrusted. She was too young. Creer made a great deal about how his woman was mature and experienced. He gave the impression she was much older. He even referred to her sometimes as my Mrs Robinson. You know, from the film."

"Yes, I understand the reference. Are you absolutely sure this is the area where Creer hid his money and his partner-in-crime lives? It's a long way from Birmingham where he was arrested."

"Without a doubt," Dick said, sipping his champagne with his little finger held aloft.

"You've been looking for attractive women in their late forties?

Maybe early fifties? I guess that sort of explains why you scared the living daylights out of Mandy Lisle."

"I quickly discounted her on the grounds of attractiveness. A very sour woman. The thought of intimate relations with her makes me shudder."

"Anything else you know about this mysterious woman that might narrow the field?" Peter asked.

"The Creer's woman loves horses."

"That doesn't really help around here. Anything else?"

"No. That's about it," Dick replied.

"Where does your friendship with Gladys fit in to all this? Does she know something about Creer's attachment to this area?"

"Gladys is a most splendid woman who has been most helpful to me in many ways, but no, I don't believe she is any way connected to that vile creature."

"You're sure of that? Have you asked her?"

"There is no need. Gladys is an honest, upright lady of this community. To suggest she would have dealings with filth like Creer is a slur on her good name."

"Does she know why you are here snooping about?"

Dick's silence answered the question.

"A lady in the village saw you poking about in the grass in Lower Woods. Have you heard the money is buried somewhere out there?"

"That nosey old battle-axe. She could also be discounted on sight as being equally unsuitable." Dick took a final sip of his champagne and placed the glass in the centre of the table. "A very drab and mean-spirited soul."

Although Peter ignored the comment, he agreed with the sentiment. "What were you looking for in the woods?"

"Mushrooms, like I told her at the time."

Peter stood. "I'm sorry, Dick, but I am needed back at the station. If Gladys hasn't reappeared by this evening, by all means, give me a call."

"You're not sending out a search party now despite all the evidence she has been abducted?" Dick asked.

"I'm not convinced you are being totally honest with me and in any event, there is no evidence she's been taken by anyone. I'm busy with a murder and a missing person enquiry."

Dick stood; the sound of his chair being scraped across the floor gained the attention of other drinkers. In a loud voice, he boomed, "My senses have never failed me. They are telling me something dreadful has happened to Gladys. I feel positive, time is of the essence. If you do not act with all due haste, you will have blood on your hands. I must demand my concerns are put on record and some action is taken now."

Peter calmly rested his hands on the back of a chair and said, "I'll register her as a missing person myself if she remains missing, but there is nothing I can do until a reasonable amount of time has elapsed. Unless, of course, you can tell me something that would link Gladys to Creer."

"You promised if I told you the truth you'd help me search for Gladys," Dick protested.

"I did, so maybe you could start answering my questions. How are you so sure Creer is in the area? Why did you break into Vivien's and Jane's houses? Have you been in contact with Creer since his escape?"

"No, I haven't, I just sense he's around, and you're going to have a double murder enquiry on your hands. You mark my words," Dick said. "While I wait for you to take this matter seriously and cease asking irrelevant questions, what do you suggest I do in the meantime?"

"Relax, stay here for another drink or check the other pubs in the area. It's really up to you." Peter felt a tug on his trouser leg. Looking down at Colin he said, "Maybe you could use Colin to track her scent. Now unless you're going to tell me about the break-ins, I really must get going."

Peter walked back to the station shaking his head. Before entering he called Glenys Pitman. "Hello, Glenys. As I'm sure you're aware, we have had your Druid priest in for questioning. If I came over now, could you show me where he was when you came across him looking for mushrooms?"

Eric Sykes looked up from behind the desk when he entered the station. "Everything sorted, sir? Did you find his Gladys?"

Peter sighed. "She'll be swaying on a bar stool somewhere. Or lying in a ditch to sleep it off. I'm off on a mushroom hunt once I collect my car keys."

"Magic ones?"

"Probably."

TWENTY-TWO

Lucy Bassett had arranged for her and her daughter to stay at Kathy's home during the search. At times her sister-in-law could be infuriating, but she always came through whenever there was a family drama.

Lucy drove the short distance in a mud-splattered land rover with Fiona and Abbie following. Fiona kept a safe distance behind, partly to avoid the spray of mud coating the windscreen when Lucy mounted the greasy grass verges without slowing, every time they met another vehicle. She also wanted to avoid the black smoke the old vehicle's exhaust pipe coughed out at regular intervals.

They pulled up outside a rank of terraced stone cottages overlooking a duck pond in the village of Alderston. Lucy leapt from the car and lit a cigarette, leaving Fiona and Abbie to encourage Ellen to leave the safe interior of the car. Fiona opened the land rover door as Ellen stayed huddled in the back seat clutching her bundle of rags.

"Come on, Ellen. Let's go and see Aunty Kathy. It's too cold out here for you both," Lucy called, from her seat on the garden wall.

Ellen's eyes widened, and she clutched the rags a little tighter. "Can't we go back home? Strange environments scare her."

"It's only for a short while, and Kathy isn't a stranger," Fiona said.

From her perch on the wall, through a cloud of smoke, Lucy called, "Come along, darling. She's family. I expect she has the house nice and cosy for us. She may even have a treat for you. Do you remember how much you liked coming here to visit when you were a little girl?"

Slowly, with a look of trepidation, Ellen unclicked the seat belt and swung her legs from the truck to the pavement.

"That's my good girl," Lucy cooed.

Fiona stepped up to hold Ellen's elbow to steady her.

"I can manage," Ellen snapped. "Perhaps you could carry the changing bag. It's on the back seat."

Lifting it, Fiona said, "It's very heavy for a couple of nappies. Ellen? Did the officers check your bag before we left?"

Ellen snatched the bag from her. "Yes, they did." Tears pricking, she added, "They tipped the contents on the table and touched everything. They put their dirty stinking hands all over my Future's precious things."

"Lucy! Ellen!" Kathy appeared on her front door steps. She beamed at Fiona. "How lovely to see you again." Wearing a nurse's uniform, she bounced down the stone steps that led from the cottage. Placing herself between the two women with her arms around their waists, she propelled Lucy and Ellen towards her open front door. Smiling to Fiona and Abbie, she called, "Come on. Don't stand on ceremony, or you'll freeze out here. The wind is bitter today, isn't it?"

The cottage was tiny but warm and quaint with uneven floors and latticed windows. They were led into a cramped living room. The low sofa and two small armchairs that took up most of the available space were mismatched and covered with an assortment of bright throws and cushions. The arms, where they protruded from the throws, were comfortably worn.

Trying to ignore the smell of wet dog and damp earth, Fiona perched on the end of an armchair, her knees touching Ellen's who sat on the end of the sofa next to her mother. The heat from the crackling real fire felt stifling and oppressive in such a small space. Even as she wriggled from her jacket, she felt her face flush in the heat.

Above the fireplace was an original painting depicting a young girl leaping over a massive hawthorn hedge astride a huge brown horse. Fiona said, "That's quite a dramatic picture," nodding towards the canvas.

"That's Kathy when she was younger. She was always a good horsewoman," Lucy said, without looking up at the painting. "That was taken during her wonder years, but she's still the darling of the hunting set. Before we moved down here, Ellen used to visit during the summer holidays and ride Kathy's pony, Jet." Twisting in her seat to face her daughter, Lucy asked, "Do you remember Jet? Such a sweet little thing."

Ellen continued to ignore Lucy.

Lucy took her daughter's hand, and asked, "Are you feeling okay?"

"I enjoy horse riding," Abbie said, in an attempt to draw Ellen from her near-catatonic state with some success.

"Do you event?" Ellen asked.

"Yes. We qualified for the Grass Roots this year. I'm so looking forward to it," Abbie replied, proudly.

"Which section?" Ellen asked.

Before Abbie could reply, Lucy said, "Maybe we could go and watch? It won't be crowded like the main event."

Fiona left them to their horsey conversation and followed the sound of the clatter of crockery to find Kathy in the kitchen. "Would you like some help?"

"No dear, I'm fine. I'll just get these snacks together for you all, and then I must get to work."

Fiona slid onto a stool in the corner of the room. A black terrier trotted over to give her a cautionary sniff before returning to its bed in front of the Aga.

"Where's DCI Hatherall today?" Kathy asked.

"He's busy elsewhere. Could I ask you a few questions before you leave?"

Kathy briefly stopped buttering the fresh bread. Restarting, she said without turning, "I suppose you want to know whether I think Ian is capable of murdering two women. Before what happened with Ellen I would have laughed at the suggestion. They were such a happy family. Always completely devoted to Ellen, of course. Partly due to the problems Lucy had getting pregnant in the first place. I think they knew they wouldn't be so lucky again. She became their miracle baby." Kathy stared out of the kitchen window. "Such happy days," she said, wistfully. "It all seemed so simple then. Ian and Lucy; me and Tom."

"And now?" Fiona asked.

Kathy placed the pile of sandwiches on a tray with the selection of homemade cakes and cookies. Wiping her hands on a dishcloth, she pulled out a second stool and climbed onto it opposite Fiona. "Ian is a good, honest, hard-working man who has had more than his fair share of heartbreak. It has made him bitter, but he's still a good man underneath." She gave a heavy sigh before continuing. "Right from the beginning, Ian refused to accept the truth. He always insisted Ellen was his little angel and an unwilling victim in the Creer fiasco. Which I'm sorry to say isn't exactly the truth. She wasn't an evil child or anything like that, but she was very spoilt and willful. Always determined to have her own way and damn the consequences. She'd learnt from practising on her father how to twist men around her little finger and persuade them to do her bidding. The combination of Robbie and her was a disaster waiting to happen."

"You mean Rob Creer?"

"Yes, only he used to call himself Robbie back then. I always found him to be polite and considerate whenever he came calling for her. It only goes to show I guess how appearances can be so deceiving."

Fiona put her hand up to stop Kathy. "Hang on a minute. I'm confused. I thought Ellen and Creer met up in Birmingham. I had no idea he had a prior connection to this area."

"Oh? I thought you already knew. Sorry, I should have explained, but I assumed Lucy had already told you."

"Perhaps you could explain, now."

Kathy quickly checked the time before continuing, "Ian was never happy about the relationship between Robbie and Ellen, even before any of us knew what they were really up to. When he discovered the age difference, he sent Ellen down here for the summer in the hope the relationship would fizzle out before it got going. Robbie had different ideas and came down every weekend to visit. Although he was ten years older than Ellen, he had a small lost boy look about him, and those eyes of his were something else."

"He stayed here with Ellen?"

"Good Lord no. Lucy would have killed me, let alone Ian. He came down during the daytime only and presumably went back to Birmingham afterwards. Have you met him?"

"No, I've only seen photographs of him."

"The pictures the newspapers had of him bore no resemblance to the quiet young man who came here. He was far more handsome and charismatic, for a start." Laughing Kathy added, "I could have fallen for him myself if I was a little younger. Whenever I saw them together, I thought of him as the ice against Ellen's fire. In my opinion, it was the combination of their personalities that caused the sparks to fly. Always egging each other on, challenging one another."

"Hang on. Are you trying to suggest Ellen had a far more active role in his crimes? Why wasn't that picked up by the police at the time?"

"Initially that's exactly the way the police and the media interpreted it. They only toned down their claims when it became clear just how damaged Ellen was in the car accident. Plus of course, she was barely sixteen, and there was a line of fully grown adults admitting they'd been manipulated and tricked by Robbie. Ian, of course, always insisted Ellen was an unwilling pawn in an adult's game, and eventually, the police let the matter drop."

"Accident?" Fiona queried. "I understand there was nothing accidental about it. He drove his car directly at her at speed and left her dying in the road."

"I'm only saying what I thought back then, and that was the two of them made an extremely bad combination. He was prepared to do anything for her, and she was always very demanding. Anyway, why am I rambling on? It was Ian you were asking about. Well over the years, his anger and denial have eaten away at him. I know from Lucy, the marriage is in tatters, and she is a nervous wreck most of the time. I wouldn't be surprised if she walks out the door one day and doesn't come back. I couldn't blame her if she did. Ian refuses to see sense where Ellen is concerned. From the second she was born, he cared about nothing else. Not even Lucy. The torture of the loss he feels has twisted him beyond all recognition to the carefree man he was before. Under the right circumstances, I wouldn't like to say what he's capable of."

A piercing wailing sound startled Fiona, and she jumped down from the stool. Kathy merely rolled her eyes. "Oh dear. I wondered what has set her off this time."

Fiona was about to question her further, but glancing at her watch, Kathy jumped nimbly from her own stool.

"Goodness! Is that the time. I have to rush, or I'll be late for work." Grabbing her car keys from the side cabinet, she called, "Nice to meet you, dear. Can I leave you to hand around the food?"

The screeching was amplified as Fiona opened the door to the small living room. Ellen was violently rocking while screaming, "She wants to take my Future," over and over again. Abbie was trying to calm the girl while her mother stood in the corner of the room looking horrified.

"Lucy!" Fiona said, quickly crossing the room. "Where are the sedatives the doctor prescribed?"

Lucy pointed to the bag on the floor next to the sofa. "In there."

Fiona snatched up the bag and rifled through the contents as the wails from Ellen became louder. "Whereabouts? No, hang on. I've got them," Fiona said, reading the instructions on the side of the bottle. "Lucy, can you bring in a glass of water, please?"

The first glass of water was snatched out of Fiona's hand and hurled across the room, shattering against the far wall. Fiona and Abbie struggled to restrain Ellen while Lucy left the room to collect another glass. Fiona made sure she kept a firm hold of the second glass as the two women forced Ellen to swallow the two tablets. Holding onto the glass while Ellen took quick sips of water, Fiona wondered if the girl could successfully sue the pair of them for assault.

It seemed like forever, but after about half an hour, Ellen visibly relaxed. A short while later, her eyes glazed over and she started to doze. The second time her head jerked forwards, waking her with a start, Fiona said, "Why don't you go upstairs for a lie-down? I'll look after your baby Future while you rest."

Despite hardly being able to keep her eyes open, Ellen held tight to her bundle of rags. "I'm fine. I need to stay alert, so she doesn't try to steal my Future from me."

"Who wants to steal her?"

Ellen tapped the side of her nose before looking down lovingly at her precious bundle.

"We're police officers, so we wouldn't allow anything to happen to her," Fiona said.

Even as Ellen shook her head, her eyes had lost focus and were closing to narrow slits.

"You look exhausted. Why don't you leave your Future under our protection and take a brief rest?" Fiona persisted.

Ellen staggered to her feet. Stumbling towards the door, she said, "Perhaps you're right. I'm going for a lie-down, but baby stays with me." Yawning, she added with a quick glance towards her mother, "Please don't light up your stinking cigarettes while I'm gone. The smoke will linger, and it's bad for her tiny lungs."

Lucy followed her daughter from the room. "I'm popping out the back door for a cigarette."

Once they were alone, Fiona said to Abbie, "Check through that changing bag thoroughly. And open any containers. I'll keep Lucy chatting for as long as I can."

Fiona found Lucy sitting on a rickety, homemade swing attached to an ancient old oak tree that stood proudly in the centre of the neat rear garden. Fiona leaned against the trunk while Lucy gently swung herself forwards and backwards.

Lucy placed her feet on the ground to halt the swing and light her cigarette. She closed her eyes and took a deep drag. With smoke curling from her nose and mouth, she gave a tiny sigh. "That feels better." She looked down at her feet and gave a sad smile. "I remember when Ellen's little legs couldn't reach the ground. This swing was made for Ellen, you know. It used to hang in our garden up north." Nodding towards the cottage, she said, "They never had children, and after our Tom died, Kathy never remarried. I don't think she ever completely got over the shock."

"What happened?"

"Poor Tom. He had a heart attack while playing rugby. Never had a day ill in his life and then poof, gone without any warning. Kathy was devastated. They'd been childhood sweethearts all through school. She went to pieces and then decided to move down here to make a fresh start working as a hunt groom, up at the big house. I don't know if it was because Ellen looked a bit like Tom or Kathy had decided without Tom she'd never have a family of her own, so hijacking my daughter was her best option. Either way for a while the two of them became quite close. At one time I resented her as I thought she was trying to take Ellen as her own. She taught her to ride and bought her a little pony."

"That was very kind of her," Fiona said.

"Yes, it was, but at the time I thought differently. Ellen was being difficult. I thought it was just typical of Kathy wanting to take what somebody else had. All water under the bridge now. She's been fantastic the last couple of years. I don't know how I would have coped without her help and support."

"What did you mean earlier by typical of Kathy?"

"Oh, something of nothing. You know what it's like when you're younger. Reading all sorts of fanciful things into quite innocent situations. It was only my imagination running away with me."

"Humour me. What did your imagination say to you?" Fiona asked.

Lucy stopped the swing and stared into the distance with a half-smile on her face. "Oh, you know, childish things. Believing she wanted to take everything away from me. We used to go around in a foursome before Tom died. They were such happy days, and I thought of Kathy like a sister as well as my best friend. It was all so perfect I should have known something would come along and ruin our happiness."

Kathy concentrated on picking at a slither of rotten wood in the swing seat. "There was an incident a few years after Tom died. Kathy was drunk and tried to seduce Ian." Lucy threw her head back and laughed. "She'd be welcome to him now."

"Is it possible Kathy knows where Ian is?"

"Doubt it. They don't get along too well these days. Her attempts at seduction left an awkwardness between them. You know how those things go. He also had grown to look upon her as almost a sister. We were all so close, but then her actions destroyed all the trust between us. You either chose to get over a betrayal like that and put it behind you like I have, or you allow it to fester away at the back of your mind. I'm not sure which of us managed to scare the living daylights out of Ian the most. Kathy's come-on or my furious reaction at the time. Anyway, it's not important now, and a lot has changed since then."

"How much do you see of Kathy?" Fiona asked.

"She pops in most days. She knows how isolated and trapped I feel, so she checks in to see if I need to get away for a few hours and she'll sit with Ellen." Lucy stubbed out the cigarette with her foot and resumed swinging. She put her feet down to bring the swing to an abrupt halt. "Ian doesn't really like her at the farm, so she mostly comes over when he's not around, or spends her time in Ellen's little flat."

"Because of her advances on him?"

Lucy shook her head and lit another cigarette. "There was a big falling out right before Ellen's incident. Ian found out Kathy had allowed Creer to visit Ellen down here when she knew we were trying to split them up. Then to make things worse, Ellen decided the pony wasn't exciting enough, and she took out Kathy's old horse, the one in the painting. Only it was ancient and semi-retired by then. Ellen tried to jump a hedge like in the picture.

The horse fell and injured itself. Kathy paid a fortune on vet bills trying to save it, but eventually, it had to be put to sleep. Kathy loved that horse. Initially when everything happened...well, let's just say she wasn't supportive to start with. Whether she really meant it or not I don't know, but Ian claimed he overheard her saying, 'serves the high and mighty little madam right.'"

"Ah. I see. But it's good you've settled your differences. Was Tom your brother or Ian's?" Fiona asked.

Lucy pushed herself higher and higher on the swing, leaning back to let her hair fall back like a child. When the swing slowed, she said, "Mine. I still miss him every day."

Fiona shifted uncomfortably, "I'm sorry."

Lucy waved her concern away. "It was terribly sad, but a long time ago. I guess now I have a greater understanding of how my parents behaved afterwards."

After a respectful silence, Fiona asked, "Does Ellen always keep hold of her pretend baby?"

"Pretty much. She made it after she was told she'd lost her real baby."

"I thought it was taken from her?" Fiona caught the look of guilt and regret in Lucy's eyes before she turned her head away. "Did Creer know she was pregnant with his baby?"

Lucy shook her head. "Nobody knew outside of the family. She couldn't have cared for it herself, and we thought we were doing the right thing under the circumstances."

"It?"

"He would have been a constant reminder for all of us and would have created a permanent link with Creer. Thinking back, I realise I shouldn't have humoured her with the substitute. Maybe if I'd been stronger and taken it from her, it wouldn't have become such a crutch. Without it, she might have faced up to reality a bit better. It seemed to give her so much comfort at the time I didn't have the heart to say anything. Kathy said it couldn't do any harm. And now it's too late."

"You look as exhausted as Ellen. Why don't you use the time she's out for the count to have a rest yourself?" Fiona suggested.

"I might just do that. Silly, really. I was up half the night cleaning. If my things were going to be gone through I at least wanted them clean and in order."

"Let's go back in out of the cold. You go on up to one of the bedrooms, and I'll check in on Ellen."

TWENTY-THREE

Fiona crept to the side of Ellen who was curled up in a foetal position on top of the bedclothes. She was half lying on the bundle of rags but had loosened her grip on them. Fiona held her breath as she gently pulled them from underneath Ellen's sleeping body. She stopped in her tracks when Ellen moaned in her sleep and adjusted her position, rolling over and trapping Fiona's hand. Slowly she released her hand before rushing downstairs to the kitchen.

Abbie interrupted her search through the kitchen drawers. "What are you doing?"

"I'm looking for a pair of scissors and a needle and thread," Fiona said, continuing her search. "Did you find anything in the changing bag?"

"Just baby stuff. The weight was from a bunch of hardback storybooks. There's something I wanted to ask you about."

Fiona moved from the drawers beside the sink to the cutlery drawers. "Great! Scissors." She looked around the room before heading towards a small drawer built into the breakfast bar behind the stools. "Go on. What did you want to ask?"

Hesitantly Abbie said, "When we were struggling with Ellen, I noticed some bruising on your arms."

Fiona sensed Abbie following her around the room and breathing down her neck. Feeling uncomfortable she tried to push herself closer towards the side cabinets. "Oh, those. They're nothing…I banged myself. You know how clumsy I can be," she replied, riffling through the drawer.

"They looked like finger marks. Like someone had grabbed hold of you. I wondered if you wanted to talk about it."

"Nothing to talk about," Fiona said, keeping her back to Abbie. "I did it at a drama workshop. We were role-playing… Bingo! Needle and cotton." She turned to find Abbie directly in front of her blocking her path. Sidestepping towards the kitchen window away from her and raising an arm to keep Abbie back, she said, "Sorry, I need more light."

Fiona dragged a kitchen stool with her and, sitting facing the window, she carefully started to unpick the stitching along the side of the dirty rag doll. She inserted her finger into the small hole she'd made and felt around in the stuffing.

Abbie appeared at her shoulder and said, "What are you doing?"

"Talking to Kathy and Lucy about how she carries this thing with her everywhere gave me an idea." A satisfied smile appeared on Fiona's face. "I think … I can feel something." She forced her thumb inside the doll and triumphantly pulled out a small key. "Look what we have here!"

"A key!"

Fiona put her fingers to her lips and pointed upstairs. She whispered, "Can you get my bag from the other room?"

When Abbie returned with the bag, Fiona pulled out her bunch of home and car keys. She twisted a small padlock key from the ring. "It's not quite the same size, but hopefully she won't notice." Keeping an ear out for sounds from upstairs, she quickly pushed her garden shed key into the doll, sewed up the small hole and crept back upstairs to return the doll to Ellen.

Abbie greeted her in the kitchen with a mug of hot tea. "Did you put it back without her noticing?"

Fiona closed the kitchen door behind her before taking the mug from Abbie and answering her. "Yup. We just have to keep our fingers crossed that she doesn't notice where I unpicked the stitching or that the key is slightly smaller." Taking a sip of the tea, she leaned against the kitchen work surface. "There was nothing to suggest she had ever unpicked the stitching to check on the key before, so hopefully she's not going to check on it now."

"She may have even forgotten it's there," Abbie said. "What do you think the key is for?"

"Well, I'm thinking as she calls the doll her future it is the key for a box that contains all the money Rob Creer stole. She is convinced Creer will be returning to collect it. When we get back to the station, could you pull up all the very early media coverage on Creer? We've been concentrating on the reports around the time of his trial and conviction. I'm especially interested in what was being reported before he was captured. Earlier Kathy was suggesting Ellen was a partner in crime rather than an innocent victim who got caught up in things. As she was pregnant with his child, I'm tempted to agree with her interpretation of the relationship."

"It took both of us to restrain Ellen when she was freaking out, and we're both pretty fit. Do you think she was responsible for the attack on Vivien and the disappearance of Jane?"

Fiona blew out her cheeks as she considered the possibility. "I wouldn't want to call it at this stage. Whatever else goes on in her head, I do think she genuinely believes Rob Creer is going to appear and whisk her away at some point." Fiona rubbed the side of her face. "On one hand, the key was hidden in the doll sometime after the accident, which does indicate some logical thought was going on. But on the other hand, to keep up such a façade in front of her parents that she's not quite right would be cruel beyond belief."

Both women looked towards the door at the sound of a creaking floorboard from upstairs. Fiona eased open the kitchen door an inch and put her ear to the crack. "I think it was just the old house settling down. Will you be okay here while I nip outside to call Peter to update him? I want to get permission to ask the search team to concentrate on Ellen's living quarters rather than the main house. I don't want either of them to wake up and overhear me."

Abbie nodded. "Of course. But when you get back, I would like to know a little more about how you got those bruises on your arm. I don't buy it was at a drama group meeting."

TWENTY-FOUR

Dick cursed, finally accepting his small stash of marijuana was gone. He sat heavily on the narrow bed in the back of his camper van and looked about at the mess he'd made during his frantic search. With his massive hands on his knees, he let his head fall forwards and down. *Goddamn crooked police. I'll have a word with Gladys when I see her. Her faith in that young man, Peter, is totally unfounded. He's as obstinate and small-minded as the rest of them.*

He looked up as Colin trotted over to him wagging her tail. He gave her a scratch behind the ears, and she dropped her head in his lap. "What are we to do, old girl?" he asked, which resulted in Colin wagging her tail harder.

"Should we up and leave? Move on to the new adventures out there that are anticipating our arrival? Maybe we could look our old pal Bob up? What do you think?"

Colin ceased wagging her tail and looked up at him with steady trusting eyes.

"You're quite correct, old thing. We can't simply desert her. That wouldn't be the done thing at all. It certainly wouldn't be cricket, would it?"

Colin wagged her tail in a slow rhythm but continued to look directly into Dick's eyes.

"What are we to do?" Dick repeated, his head drooping towards his knees again in a perfect picture of despair. "What are we to do?"

Colin forcefully snuffled her snout deeper into Dick's lap.

Dick abruptly leapt to his feet, banging his head on the ceiling of the camper van. Rubbing his head, he danced from one foot to the other. "Of course! Of course! Oh, silly unworthy me. What was I thinking? You know where she is, don't you? You can lead me to her!"

Pushed backwards from Dick's lap, Colin sneezed and appeared to nod assent. Dick flung his arms around the dog's neck. "You wonderful creature! Where would I be without you? Come, we must make provisions for our epic rescue."

Preparations consisted of donning a deerstalker hat and a heavy tweed jacket. In one pocket he stuffed a half bottle of whisky and in another a carving knife from the cutlery drawer. He pulled one of Gladys' sweaters from the laundry basket, scrunched it into a ball and held it in front of Colin's nose for a timed thirty seconds. In the porch, he reluctantly undid his open-toed sandals and stepped into a pair of wellingtons. He forced the sweater into Colin's snout again and instructed, "Go find her, girl."

Colin bounded ahead, sniffing at the hedgerows as they headed towards Hinnegar Woods. "Good girl. I know with your help I'll soon be by the side of my beloved. In the wink of an eye, we'll be reunited."

In the woods, the ground became increasingly boggy as they slopped their way through water-filled tractor tracks. A light drizzle settled in, making the going increasingly slippery and heavy going. Every time Dick slipped, it splashed brown sludge over the top of his boots. His enthusiasm for the adventure diminishing with every step.

"Are you sure she took this treacherous path that lies before us?"

Colin jogged back to her master wagging her tail, so they proceeded onwards.

Colin veered off the path and cantered up a steep bank. Puffing and panting, leaning heavily on his staff, Dick clambered up behind her. As he reached the peak, he used exposed tree roots to pull himself to the top. He called to Colin who had disappeared through thick undergrowth. "Colin, are you quite sure about the course we are taking?"

Colin barked enthusiastically from somewhere on the other side. Dick resigned himself to forcing his large frame through the bramble. He pulled down his sleeves to cover his hands, already scratched and bleeding, and propelled himself forwards. With his head bent down, he powered forwards in a style that would win him a place on any international rugby team.

On the other side, a grass-covered clearing about the size of a rugby pitch spread out before him. Under the cover of the trees, he'd been so intent on keeping his footing he hadn't realised the light persistent drizzle had turned to heavy rain. Warm from his climb up the bank, he didn't feel the cold, but he did feel the rain start to seep through his clothes. Colin sat contentedly by a fallen tree wagging her tail, oblivious to her soaking wet, mud-drenched fur.

Doubts of Colin's tracking ability entered Dick's mind for the first time. Wearily he pulled the balled jumper out from under his jacket and held it out to Colin. With rain dripping from his nose, his heart fell as Colin took one sniff before relieving herself on the fallen log and sitting down with a pleased look on her face.

His hopes destroyed, Dick sat on the log and took a long drink from the whisky bottle. Screwing the lid back on, he said without conviction, "Find, girl. Find."

Colin walked in a small circle and sat back down. Feeling wet, cold and miserable, Dick accepted defeat. He gave Colin a pat. "You did your best, old girl. No one can ask more than that. I was in the wrong to expect too much of you. Please don't feel as though you failed me."

He unscrewed the lid of the whisky bottle and took another gulp. Colin gave him a hard nudge with her nose.

"Careful! You nearly made me spill some of this delightful amber liquid from the gods." Colin sat squarely in front of Dick intently watching him.

Replacing the lid, Dick noticed the dog's intense stare. "Ah, I see. I'm afraid this particular gift from the gods is only to be consumed by two-legged creatures. You, my faithful friend, have four." Patting the bottle, he added, "You see, my friend, this liquid can make the control of two legs a very tricky business, especially for those who lack prior experience of the perfect blend of malts. I dread to think of the outcome should the recipients have the responsibility of four legs to control."

Dick shivered despite the whisky warming his insides. He stroked Colin's head. "I'll sit here a while to catch my breath and lubricate my limbs. Afterwards, we'll make our way home empty handed but not yet defeated. We'll just have to think of another plan."

Colin ran behind the log and returned with a length of branch. She dropped it at Dick's foot and took a step back.

Dick watched her eyes flick forwards and back from the branch to him. "Although I'm not blaming you for your failure to track Gladys, I am not minded to reward your efforts with a game of fetch."

Colin gently picked up the branch and plonked it in Dick's lap.

"No," Dick said firmly. "This is not a game. I don't want the wet, dirty thing." Only when he looked down, it wasn't wet. He guessed Colin must have pulled it out from under the shelter of the log. About to throw it over his shoulder, he noticed the dark stain on one end. Looking closer and giving it a good sniff, he realised it was blood. Remembering the last time, he innocently picked up a murder weapon, he instantly threw it as far away as he could. "Leave it, Colin," he shouted to the dog, who ignored him and returned it to Dick's feet. Dick edged away along the log while Colin pushed the branch along the floor after him.

Looking anywhere except at the offending branch, Dick spotted a glass discarded in a clump of grass. Picking it up, he closely examined the lipstick mark clinging to the rim. "This I believe is the colour my beloved favours." He patted Colin with his free hand. "By Jove, Colin, I think we're on to something here." He closed his eyes and concentrated hard on sensing whatever message the glass might have for him.

He was interrupted by a low growl from Colin and a tug on the hem of his robe. "Not now, Colin. I'm sending my mind out to seek Gladys." He tried again but the tug at his clothes became more insistent. He opened his eyes at the point he was about to be dragged from the log. "What is it you wish to convey to me, Colin?"

Colin let go of his robe and darted towards the undergrowth they'd come from. When Dick didn't immediately follow, he ran back to him and gave another tug on his robe. With his belief in the dog's powers fortified by the recent discovery, Dick slipped the glass into his jacket pocket and followed the dog. Clambering down the bank he'd struggled to ascend earlier, he saw Colin lying low at the bottom. Reaching her, he crouched down next to the dog as she gave another low growl. "What is it that so offends you, old thing?" With his head held low to the dog as if expecting a whispered reply, he heard someone walking past above them.

Dick dropped to the floor. Pressing himself against the muddy bank, he tried to slither his way upwards to get a glance of the stranger without being seen.

By the time he reached the top, he was plastered in mud, and the walker was long gone. Dick scrabbled to his feet and with Colin trotting at his heels, walked slowly into the clearing. He checked the ground for fresh footprints. The wet ground was so churned up it was hard to tell which direction the mysterious walker had taken. Colin was generally a bold dog who wouldn't hide away from strangers, so her reaction to the walker was cause for concern.

Dick closed his eyes and pressed his forefingers to his temples to divine which path the stranger had taken. Deciding to take the path to the left of the clearing, he started to move in that direction. Colin ran around him in circles making it difficult to make any headway and impossible to plant his staff in front of him.

"What has gotten into you today?" Dick waved his staff to shoo Colin away before slapping his own forehead. "Oh, I am a foolish old man. You have proven your worthiness in our search, yet I continue to doubt you." He turned to face the opposite direction.

"Lead on, my valiant champion. Where you lead, I shall dutifully follow."

Colin gambolled happily along a narrow track with Dick panting behind as it sloped upwards. He stopped at the brow of the rise to find a handkerchief to mop his brow and catch his breath. Through the trees below, he could make out the roof and chimney of a small cottage. "We must move towards the property with great stealth, Colin, as we do not know what evils lie within." He took a few cautious steps before he tripped on an exposed tree root and rolled and slid down the embankment. He finally came to a rest in a heap next to the tumbled-down remains of a dry stone wall.

Pulling twigs and rotten leaves from his beard and robes, he squinted at the forlorn and desolate cottage. With his finger on his lips, he tiptoed the short distance to the garden gate with Colin a few steps behind. The ornate metal gate creaked ominously and closed behind Dick with a loud clang after he released it. Colin chose to hop over the wall into the abandoned garden covered with fallen leaves. Dick walked around the cottage, checking each mullioned window. Curtains were drawn at every one, preventing him from seeing inside. The path to a weather-beaten back door was ankle deep in damp leaves where they had been blown into the alcove. A brisk draft swirled around Dick's legs, lifting his bedraggled robes as he gave a firm tug on the door handle. When it refused to budge, Dick considered using his trusty staff to break a window. He reasoned being re-arrested for vandalism and house-breaking wouldn't help the situation. He called, "Gladys, my darling. Are you within," to no reply.

He smoothed down his hair and jacket and headed around the side of the house to the front door. He rapped three times on the door and called out, "Gladys!" a little louder. The cottage remained stubbornly silent as a heavy downpour of rain arrived. The doorway offered little shelter as the driving rain started to gust horizontally towards the cottage. A very unhappy Colin sat in a puddle waiting for Dick's next command.

Turning his back on the cottage and blinking the rain from his eyes, Dick leaned heavily on his staff. "My clever faithful hound, this is the plan. We will return home at this juncture. Once we are again dry and presentable, we will inquire of local establishments of the owner of this abandoned property. Dependant on the information we receive, we will consider our options. If the gods decree we should return, we will do so under cover of darkness and I'll ensure we are better prepared for the elements. If Gladys is within, I'll find a way to gain entry."

Colin gave a sharp bark in reply.

"No Colin. I am grateful for your assistance, but I am not minded to inform the local constabulary of our findings at this point in time."

TWENTY-FIVE

Peter paced the small office space. "I can't believe they found nothing at all at Park Farm."

"They've still got all the outhouses to check. They might find something yet," Fiona replied.

"And that's a double-edged sword. Any word on when they're going to be finished? I can't see Creer trying to contact Ellen to recover this key until they're all clear of the property. I'm not even totally convinced the key does have anything to do with him."

Fiona shrugged. "Do you want another coffee?"

"I've a feeling I'll want something stronger once that psychiatrist has finished interviewing Ellen. If she maintains the same responses as she did with you, and Doctor Carney says her diminished understanding is genuine, then we're not any closer to knowing what is going on. If the murder and disappearance is related to Creer's escape, I still think our best chance is trying to get the full story from Dick. I wonder if it is worth watching the area where Glenys Pitman saw him acting suspiciously. If the money is buried somewhere out in Lower Woods, then the key could be a complete red herring."

Fiona checked her watch. "The interview should be nearly over by now. Do you want me to go over there to ask Doctor Carney to come and speak with you once he's finished?"

"You could do," Peter replied, continuing his pacing. "We need to get something positive. We're not even absolutely sure whether Jane Salt is running around alive and well shacked up with an escaped criminal or has been killed or is being held captive by a revengeful father." He thrust the photograph of Creer into Fiona's hands. "Do you see the appeal of the man? Because I sure as hell can't see what a professional woman would be prepared to give up everything for. Can you?"

Fiona gave the picture a cursory glance. "With men like him, it's often more than their looks. It's their whole personality and the way they make women feel. It could be a certain look he has perfected, or maybe he is very good at working out what a woman wants to hear and then says it by the bucket load. He could get to them by playing the vulnerable, sensitive soul misunderstood by the world. Or he could play the rough diamond they think they can mould." She handed back the picture as brusquely as she was given it. "Who knows? But you can't just look at a photograph to find out."

"Well, thanks for that insight. You seem touchy about the subject?"

"Not really. Anyhow, didn't Creer con men as well as women, moving comfortably within the elite circles of those he was robbing?"

Peter dropped the photograph onto his desk. "Which leaves us with a charming liar who doesn't care who he uses to get what he wants." He crossed the room and perched on the window sill.

"So, do you think Jane Salt helped Creer escape when she visited her friend in Birmingham?"

"I've looked at the timings and yes, that is what I think. The fact no one has seen him since he left the hospital suggests he was driven away and has been given a safe place to hide." Peter banged his forehead with his palm in frustration at his stupidity. "Jane lived in her partner's house. Have we checked whether she had her own property before? Maybe she held on to it and keeps it rented out."

Fiona drew a large square on the whiteboard and wrote, 'Jane—check for owned or recently rented property & search her home.'

"The home she shared with her partner, Sheila Bond?" Peter

asked.

"Might as well, if we're talking about what people will do for love. The house is big enough, and we only went into the living room and their shared bedroom."

"Except I'd stake my career on Sheila Bond's reaction to her disappearance being genuine. She's ringing the station every hour asking for an update and requesting a television appeal for her return," Peter said. "Jot down what we know for certain. Jane Salt visited Creer on a regular basis. She was in the area when he escaped, and there have been no sightings of either of them since. Dick has indicated Creer's help on the outside is an older woman, whereas Jane is a similar age to him. We know Jane tried to get access to Ellen by posing as a journalist. This does support your theory that Ellen holds the key to Creer's money and he intends to recover it."

Peter ceased pacing and sat on the window ledge overlooking Tibberton High Street. "If the key you've retrieved from the doll does unlock his fortune, how would Creer know that was where she hid it? Don't forget the doll was obtained months after Creer was captured and they had no contact with one another in the interim period. Also, if Dick is correct about the age of Creer's accomplice, then Ellen was just a minor player being used and manipulated by him, so why leave an important key in her possession?"

Fiona wrote on the board, 'Triple check no contact between Ellen & Creer after his arrest.' She tapped the pen on her chin before replying, "Jane wouldn't need to know where the key was hidden, just that she had it. Maybe she planned to gain Ellen's trust by saying she was sent by Creer and he wanted to check she'd kept the key he'd given to her?"

"When do you think he gave her the key? When she was lying in the road? Reports say he drove his vehicle directly at her. He was arrested shortly after by traffic police. The arrest was sheer luck. They only caught him because a witness to the accident contacted them with the registration number. Why would he try to kill the person he trusted to look after something so important?"

Fiona crinkled her forehead in frustration. She had been so excited by her moment of inspiration and the discovery of the key. Peter running holes through her theory showed she hadn't thought it all through properly. Maybe Julien was right when he said she wasn't as clever as she thought she was.

"There is, of course, another more feasible explanation of how the key came into her possession," Peter said, starting to pace again. "She'd been given the key sometime earlier, and Creer asked her to bring the key to him on the day of the accident. Maybe her father is correct that she went with the intention of talking him into giving himself up voluntarily, and so she left the key at home. She may not have even realised its importance. When he discovered she'd turned up without his key, he lost his temper. The witness only saw him drive his car directly towards Ellen on her bicycle. Maybe they'd already argued, and Ellen was trying to cycle away when he hit her?"

"Except it was a head-on collision," Fiona reminded him.

"He could have driven past and then turned around, or Ellen could have stopped and turned back to face him. She has no recollection of what happened, and we can't rely on Creer's explanation that she appeared out of nowhere in front of him."

"It all sounds very reasonable and logical when put like that. It could have happened that way," Fiona said. "But we can't get past the fact Creer was in hospital under guard when Vivien was attacked. Going back to your theory, are you suggesting Jane killed Vivien?"

"She could have confided in Vivien and asked her to get the key from Ellen. That could have been what they were arguing about in the pub. Jane had met her there expecting her to hand over the key. After storming out, Vivien may have waited outside for ten minutes to continue the discussion."

Fiona turned to look at the board. "There was little evidence of a struggle, and all the footprints around where Vivian was found were from a woman's shoe. We assumed they were made by Vivien walking to meet her attacker, but possibly they were

Jane's footprints."

"Except the time of death has been put at a few hours later and she had a solid alibi for that night. One that has been confirmed by her partner, who is a reputable London barrister," Peter said.

"Weren't we talking a moment ago of what people will do to protect those they love? A lover giving a false alibi is hardly unheard of. Just because they had tickets for a musical doesn't mean they definitely attended the performance," Fiona said.

"As you discovered, Jane knew there was a problem with one of the leads' voice during the performance. That indicates she was there in the audience."

"She could have picked up that information from someone else who had watched the performance. For all we know, they planned to attend the musical as part of a larger group." Fiona sighed. "We have to hope they will try to get the key from Ellen. Do you think they will?"

"Considering the amount of money we're talking about, I don't think they'll leave the country without it," Peter replied.

"You're still not convinced the key is relevant, are you?"

"Initially, I was doubtful Jane would attack an old college friend and work colleague, but you're right to point out the extremes people will go to for love." Peter rubbed his jaw. "I like your theory about the key, and we haven't anything better, but I have concerns. Mostly due to the time lapse between Creer's arrest and when she started to carry the doll around."

Peter started to count on his fingers. "One, where was the key in the interim period? Two, Ellen claims to know nothing about the key or how it got there. Three, the medical evidence suggests Ellen is telling the truth. Four, we have no idea what the key is for and finally five, how does Ian Bassett fit in to all this? He has had years of anger building up inside him, and then two women pop along who appear to be sympathetic towards the cause of all his misery. Shortly after leaving his home, one turns up battered to death, and the other disappears. Where is he now? No one has seen him since the morning he heard that Creer had escaped from Shoreham. Or are you suggesting Jane killed him as well?"

"No, I hadn't considered that."

"So, where is he?"

Before Fiona could answer, the phone rang. Peter grabbed it on the first ring and listened briefly before excusing himself and saying to Fiona, "It's Birmingham. Ian Bassett has surfaced. Go and find out what Dr Carney made of Ellen."

When Fiona returned, Peter was standing with his full attention focussed on the whiteboard. "Well?" he asked, over his shoulder.

Fiona joined him at the board. "Sorry, he had to rush off, but in his opinion, Ellen isn't capable of conducting an elaborate lie or planning anything."

"And Birmingham have confirmed Ian Bassett has been in hospital the last few days. He walked into Creer's old local and caused a fight, which just let's say didn't go too well for him. It was only when he regained consciousness anyone realised who he was. I'll let you contact his wife with the good news. I've spoken to the search team. They're ready to bag everything up and leave the farm. Are you free this evening? I think it might be worth our while to watch the farm and see if Creer does put in an appearance."

"Yeah. Sure," Fiona replied, still staring at the board.

"You don't sound too sure? Did you have other plans for the evening?"

"No, I'm free, but now you've got me doubting the importance of the key."

"I'm not saying it's not relevant, but I think we're missing something else. I have the horrid feeling it's staring us in the face, but I can't see it yet," Peter said.

"I wonder how Ellen will cope with this all going on around her. She's paranoid as it is that people want to steal her precious non-existent baby. It was her obsession with the doll that made me think it contained something else. If she really was unaware the key was hidden inside, then she could be completely innocent and simply very confused."

"Have they released her yet?"

"They were just waiting for Lucy to collect her when I left," Fiona said.

"See if you can catch Lucy before they leave and persuade her to take Ellen somewhere else tonight. The sister-in-law again? When you've done that, get on home for a break." Peter checked his watch. "I'll pick you up from yours at about six thirty."

Fiona said, "I'd better go now if I'm going to catch Lucy."

The door had hardly swung shut when Abbie Ward entered the room. "Sir, can I have a quick word? It's not exactly about work, but it's important."

"Sure, come in. What's troubling you?"

"It's a bit awkward. It's about DI Williams, Fiona. Have you noticed anything?"

"No. I don't think so."

"You work with each other every day, and I know you care for her." Abbie quickly added, "As a friend, of course."

"I'm not sure where you're going with this but hurry up and say what you're trying to say. I've things to do."

"This new boyfriend of hers…"

Peter frowned and started to back away. "I'm pretty sure I'm not the person you should be talking to about this."

Abbie took a step forward, holding her hands palm up in front of her. "Just let me finish. I think he's violent towards her. He's definitely controlling her. And yesterday I noticed bruises all down her arm. She claimed she got them in a drama workshop, but I don't believe her. I wondered if you had noticed anything."

Realising if he stepped back again he'd be trapped against his desk, Peter stood his ground and replied, "Nothing springs to mind but Fiona is a strong, modern woman. I think it's unlikely she would tolerate a violent or controlling boyfriend. She's far too smart, and if she said she received the injuries at drama, I would tend to believe her."

"Would you at least ask her about the bruising?"

Peter didn't recognise the number on his phone display but was glad of the distraction when it rang. He immediately raised his hand for Abbie to stop. "This call is important. Leave it with me."

Placing the phone to his ear, he recognised the caller straight away. "Calm down and give me the address again. We're on our way." Disconnecting the call, he ignored Abbie who hadn't retreated and rang Fiona. Turning his back on Abbie, he circled his desk while checking for a postcode for the address he'd been given and scribbling it down. He was wriggling into his jacket when Fiona answered his call.

"Fiona. Meet me in the car park straight away." Passing Abbie, he gave her the postcode and said, "A dead woman has been found at this address. Can you organise a team out there as quickly as possible?" Marching along the corridor with his phone to his ear, he said, "There's been a change of plan." He disconnected the call and rushed on taking two steps at a time on his way to the car park. Jumping into his car he punched the postcode into his navigation device.

"Peter. What's happened? Where are we going?" Fiona asked, sliding into the passenger seat. I thought I was heading home."

Peter started the engine and sped across the car park. "Remember I said Gladys had apparently gone AWOL?"

"As I recall you said she was probably drunk somewhere."

"Yeah, well it seems I was wrong about that as well. Dick has just found her out at some derelict cottage."

Fiona was pushed against the back of her seat as the car accelerated away. "Is she okay?"

"She'll live, unlike the dead woman sprawled across the kitchen floor," Peter replied.

"What? Who?"

"We'll know that when we get there but I've a nasty feeling from the description he gave it could be Jane Salt."

"If it is, that shoots a massive hole right through the middle of my thinking," Fiona said. "You were never completely convinced about Jane Salt being Vivien's attacker, were you?"

"Yes and no, to be honest." Peter swung the car hard around to the right throwing Fiona against the car door. "Sorry. I think I know a shortcut to where we're heading." Peter floored the accelerator as they raced along the main road away from Tibberton. He slowed abruptly and turned right through a narrow gap between two stone walls. The dark lane narrowed, and the jarring from the numerous potholes they hit forced Peter to slow his speed. "This will still be quicker," he said, more to convince himself than Fiona.

They passed a cottage in darkness as the single-track lane turned to little more than a footpath winding its way through a wooded area. It turned to mud with a few chippings scattered across the top surface. The car bounced and groaned as it struggled to keep traction over the undulating track with deep grooves created by quad bikes and off-road vehicles. Mud sprayed up the side of the car with only its speed keeping it going forward instead of stuttering to a halt in the deep mud.

"See," Peter said, sounding more relieved than triumphant when the navigation system located where they were. "Almost there."

After staying silent for most of the journey, Fiona said, "Do you think my reasoning was affected by my dislike of Jane?"

"What? Don't worry about that now. We all bring our preconceived ideas to the job. The fact you've recognised the possibility puts you ahead of most people."

"In other words, yes."

Peter pulled over to the side. "We'll have to walk the rest of the way." He pointed, "It's just over there, behind the trees. See?"

Stepping out of the car Fiona sunk ankle deep in mud. With cold, wet mud already circling around inside her shoes, she splashed her way around the car to join Peter.

"Come on. Hurry. For all we know, whoever killed her may be on his way back," Peter said impatiently.

"Who do you think it is? Creer?"

"I'm hoping Gladys will be able to tell us."

Slipping and sliding over a bank of mud, they could hear the distant sounds of sirens approaching from a different direction. Their moving lights confirmed they were travelling along a road rather than wading ankle-deep through mud.

They were halfway along the garden path when the front door

swung open. "Thank the heavens above and all their celestial beings it is you," Dick announced. Hearing the approaching sirens, he added, "With the cavalry taking up your rear."

"Where is she?" Peter asked, starting to jog towards the front door.

Dick pressed his back against the wall to avoid being bowled over. "Gladys is in the front room recovering from her ordeal."

"No, I mean the dead woman you say is here," Peter shouted.

Dick gave him a quizzical look. "She's quite dead, you know. Long past anything you could do for her. Her spirit has escaped into the atmosphere. She may already be recreated as we speak. A new life rising from pain and despair."

Peter pushed past Dick. "Where is she?"

"She smells quite wiffy as well," Dick said, pointing to the kitchen door. Following on behind he held his nose and added, "Rather you than me. Oh, and thank you for doing our job and discovering where a respectable member of the community was being held captive by an escaped criminal. A criminal you were supposed to be keeping safely behind lock and key." Dick stopped just inside the doorway and shook his head. "I don't know what this world is coming to or how it will all end."

"Yes, thank you," Peter said, holding his jacket sleeve over his nose as he crossed the room and knelt next to the body. He stood and nodded to Fiona, "It is Jane Salt," just as the cars could be heard arriving outside. He ushered them all out of the room. "The whole cottage will be a crime scene. We need to get out of the way and let them do their job." Addressing Dick, he said, "I'll take you and Gladys home. I'm sure you'd both prefer to answer our questions there rather than at the station."

They found Gladys sat stiffly and upright in the living room gazing into space. Peter couldn't remember a time he'd seen her so still and quiet. Her face was devoid of her usual garish make-up and had a grey pallor. Her hands were clasped tightly in her lap.

Fiona whispered in his ear, "Shouldn't we take her to hospital? She may need medical treatment."

Peter crouched down by Gladys' side. His eyes were drawn to her hands, which he noticed for the first time were distorted and swollen by arthritis. He placed his hand on hers and gently said, "Gladys. It's DCI Peter Hatherall. Are you up to answering a few questions?"

Gladys slowly turned her head to face him and gave a silent nod.

"This is important, Gladys. Other questions can wait until you've been checked over by a doctor. I need to know, who the man was who held you here was and whether he gave any indication of where he was going, and when he would be returning?"

Gladys' eyes widened, but she appeared to be looking straight through him, focussed on some unseen horror in the distance only she could see.

"Peter," Fiona interrupted. "I'd better go and let the SOCCO team in."

Peter half turned and gave her the thumbs up.

"Gladys," Peter tried again while giving her hand a quick squeeze. "It's really important we know. Then we can get you to hospital."

Gladys gave a heavy sigh and focused her eyes on Peter, narrowing them into a glare. She freed her hands from under his and pushed her hair away from her face.

"Young man! I am not going to hospital. I am as fit as a fiddle, so away with your nonsense." Dropping her hands from her hair, she said, "My hair is a frightful mess, darling. It's a hairdresser I need not a bloody quack."

Peter struggled to hide a wide smile and dropped his forehead, banging his head gently on her arm. "Good to have you back."

Smoothing her skirt, Gladys retorted, "I've been here all the time. What took YOU so long to find me?"

Standing up and manoeuvring himself onto the couch beside her, Peter said, "I'm afraid Dick must take full credit for finding you." He shook his head slightly while Gladys and Dick shared a beaming smile across the room. "Sorry to break you two lovebirds up, but we need to know if your abductor is likely to return any time soon."

Gladys shook her head. "No darling, he's not coming back. He said he was leaving me here to die a slow and painful death. I was locked in a small bedroom with a boarded-up window. Left lost and alone to meet my maker by that frightful little man."

"Did he say anything else?" Peter asked.

"Oh yes. He joked he might contact my sweet Dick. Firstly, to taunt him about how I'd run away with another. Then later once he was sure I would have died of hunger and thirst, he planned to direct him to this place. Trapped inside without sunlight or the feel of wind on my face I would have withered and died, a broken woman knowing of the pain and anguish my dear Dick was suffering."

"Thanks, that's really helpful," Peter interrupted. "Did he say where he was going?"

"No, my little sweet cherub. Only that he was going to collect what was rightfully his and leave this dreary country for warmer shores."

The door opened, and Fiona poked her head into the room. "Sir. They'd like a quick word and then would like us all out of here."

"Sure," Peter said, already halfway across the room. "Get Gladys and Dick settled in the car, and I'll meet you outside."

TWENTY-SIX

Outside the car Peter rang the station to ask for a surveillance team out at the Park Farm, warning them that Creer may be on his way. Climbing into the car, he raised a surprised eyebrow at Gladys in the front seat and looked round to see Fiona in the back with Dick.

"I get the most horrendous travel sickness if I'm not in the front," Gladys announced. "Now I trust you are a safe and experienced driver. I can't abide poor driving. It puts me all on edge." She clapped her hands twice. "Chop. Chop. We haven't all day."

Peter pulled the seat belt across himself. "Hospital or home?"

"Home, James."

Gladys started to give a running commentary on Peter's driving skills the second he pulled away. Peter held up his hand and said, "We won't be stopping long once we've seen you safely home. Our aim is to capture your abductor tonight. So maybe you could think of anything that might help us rather than worrying about my driving ability."

To distract her, stifling a chuckle, Fiona pulled up a picture of Rob Creer on her phone and passed it to Gladys. "Is that your abductor?"

Gladys studied it closely before handing it back. Peter's heart sank, and his thoughts raced when he thought for one awful moment she was going to say no. If it wasn't Creer, they were way off track.

"He has dyed his hair blond, but yes, that's the little blighter. No one could disguise those eyes of his. It's like looking into an iceberg. So cold and yet oddly suggestive of hidden depths. Depths of cruelty and evilness. But depth all the same." Gladys turned around in her seat and stroked Colin, who was taking up much of the space in the back seat. "Sorry, Dick. He told me how he had beaten poor Colin with a stick when she tried to protect me. Have you checked her over for injuries?"

"What a brave girl," Dick said, and started to prod the dog, who arched her back and delivered a string of slobber to Fiona's lap.

"Yuk!" Fiona said. "Has anyone got any tissues?"

Gladys opened the glove compartment and after a quick rummage around handed a windscreen sponge back to Fiona. "Here you are, dear. Will this do?"

"Back to your abductor," Peter said sharply. "Did he have any visitors to the cottage? Did you hear him talking to anyone?"

"Hard to tell," Gladys replied, turning to face forwards again. "I was locked away in a cold, damp room the entire time, contemplating my mortality. I didn't hear anyone else moving about, but I did hear him talking. I had the impression he was either talking to himself or possibly to imaginary friends. Although he could have been talking to someone on the telephone, I suppose." Gladys gave an exaggerated sigh. "One's imagination can play tricks when waiting in the darkness for certain death to arrive."

"Did you catch any of what he was saying?" Peter asked.

"It was all very muffled, darling, and I could only make out the odd word here and there. There were times I thought I was in the depths of hell listening to the ramblings of a madman. Several times he mentioned a stag and the devil. Oh, and he sometimes shouted, 'why can't I remember?' I've no idea what he meant. I thought maybe he'd misplaced something. His marbles probably."

"Any names mentioned?" Fiona asked.

Gladys thought for a while and then said, "Two." He regularly said, my dear, dear Janey what a disappointment you turned out to be. Other times he berated her for being so uncommunicative."

"But you never heard a woman or anyone else reply?"

"Not a dickie bird, sweet pea."

"And the other name?" Peter asked.

"He only mentioned this name the once. Let me remember the phrase he used." After a brief silence, she said, "My poor beautiful, but totally deluded, Ellen. What a cold-hearted bitch you turned out to be. Handing our baby over to strangers without a second thought. You nearly had me fooled."

"Just those two names? You're absolutely sure there wasn't a third name?"

Gladys thought a moment before replying, "Those were the only two names I heard clearly, but he rambled a lot. I couldn't make out everything he said from behind a locked door. Plus of course, darling, much of the time I was quaking with fear."

"Roughly how long ago did he leave you?"

"At least two hours ago."

TWENTY-SEVEN

When they arrived at Gladys' home, Peter ordered they stay in the car while he went inside first to check the house was safe. Fiona unbuckled her seat belt to follow him, but Peter twisted around in his seat and said, "No, you stay here and watch the front door." He held out his hand to Gladys. "Can I have your back door key?" Once he took it from her, he opened the rear passenger door on the other side. "Out, Dick. You're coming with me."

Fiona moved to the driver seat after watching Peter disappear around the side of the house and focused her attention on the front door.

"Do you think the brute is inside my home?" Gladys asked.

Keeping her eyes on the door, Fiona replied, "I wouldn't have thought so. I think Peter wanted to make absolutely sure you're both safe before we leave."

"That's awfully good of him," Gladys said. "I suppose it's the least he can do in the circumstances. I mean what would have happened to me if my wonderful, dashing Dick hadn't come searching for me?"

Fiona tried to concentrate and tune out Gladys' voice as she continued to witter away about her hero Dick. She checked her watch constantly. It didn't make any sense why Peter wanted to check the house. Creer wouldn't be wasting time here. He'd be trying to retrieve the key from Ellen. She started to tap her foot impatiently and said, "Come on, Peter."

Gladys leant across and whispered in her ear. "Do you think he's found something?"

◆ ◆ ◆

Inside, Peter directed Dick to a kitchen chair and said, "Right… talk. Where has Creer hidden the money?"

"I have no idea," Dick protested. "I can't believe after all I've done you are speaking to me in this way. You should be thanking me."

Peter turned a chair around and straddled it, facing Dick. "I've been good enough to question you away from Gladys. Why were you so sure Creer was in the area and he'd taken Gladys?" Peter held up his hand and added, "And don't give me that rubbish you received the information from some higher spirit living in the trees. I want straight answers."

Dick folded his arms. "It was just a hunch, and you gave me the idea of using Colin to track Gladys. I had no idea that was where he'd taken her. I just followed Colin."

"Ah yes. Good old Colin that never leaves your side. You even took her with you when you broke into their houses, didn't you?"

"I have no idea what you are talking about."

"No? You're quite sure about that? You see, after they were broken into, there was a smell of damp dog lingering in the house. We've collected stray dog hairs from Vivien Morse's house," Peter lied. "It will only be a matter of time before tests confirm they belong to your dog. If you hate Creer as much as you claim, tell me what you know now, and we'll have a chance of recapturing him."

"I've told you all I know."

"Or you can wait until the tests come back on those dog hairs. When they do, I'll arrest you for helping him escape, breaking and entry and possibly even murder. Your choice. What happened? Did he promise you a share but then double-crossed you?" Peter said.

"I must protest. I would never help that man."

"Tell me what you know, or God help me, I'm going to charge

you with something and get you sent back inside. This isn't a game. He could get away or harm somebody else."

"Okay. I worked in the post room in Shoreham. He received letters from women from all around the world."

"Did you hold back some of his letters and read them? Is that how you discovered he'd hidden the money around here?" Peter asked.

"Yes."

"You thought you could get to his fortune before him? That's why you broke into the houses, wasn't it? They both wrote to him, didn't they? You were looking for Creer's replies to work out where the money was hidden."

"Yes, I wanted to find his hiding place, but I didn't break into their homes," Dick insisted.

"I want the name of the third person in this area Creer wrote to."

"I swear I don't know who it is."

"Then tell me what you do know. Why were you poking around in the woods that day you claim you were looking for mushrooms?"

"A fool's errand, I'm afraid. Someone told me that was where horses went to die," Dick replied.

"What nonsense is that? You still don't seem to have grasped the seriousness of your situation. Two women are dead. Do you want to end up back inside?"

"Okay, I'll tell you everything as it happened. That way it'll be clear in my own mind. You should know, if you want to make a career out of police work, that your questioning is just confusing me. I need to centre myself." Dick closed his eyes and pressed his thumb and forefinger together on each hand which he raised to his ears and hummed a low note. He opened his eyes before saying, "I'm centred."

"Get on with it," Peter said, impatiently.

"I found a letter he accidentally left out one day. It said the safe containing all the proceeds from his illegal activities was buried with a horse and the key was being looked after. It was the middle part of a letter, and there was no address at the top of the sheet. However, the writer mentioned attending a village day and playing a game of boules in Supworth. After that, I tried to get a look at all of his letters, but I was only rostered to the post room on Mondays and Fridays. Through persistence, I discovered two of his ladies, Jane and Vivien, lived near only some fifteen miles from that very same village. Certainly, close enough to visit for a day-out. You know, Creer didn't even write the replies half the time? He got other inmates to write them for him."

"Can you keep to the relevant facts and tell me what happened? Did you kill Vivien when she wouldn't tell you what you wanted to know?"

"I swear to God I didn't kill anyone. I never even met or spoke to her or that other one. Had I known who they were when they argued in the pub, I would have intervened immediately. I can't believe I missed that opportunity."

"Yet another strange coincidence in the life of Dick," Peter said sarcastically.

"Yes, that happens to me a lot. I wanted to find the money and gloat over it, but I'd never kill for it. You must believe me."

"Luckily for you, I do believe that much. Is there anything else, no matter how small or apparently insignificant you can tell me to help us locate Creer?"

Dick shook his head. "Sorry, that's everything."

◆ ◆ ◆

"What's taking them so long?" Gladys asked for the fifth time.

Before Fiona could reply the downstairs hall-way light came on, and Peter made his way to the car. Leaning on the roof, he said to Gladys, "I know this sounds a bit random, but what do people do with the body when a horse dies?"

Gladys shrieked, "What's happened to Cara," and tried to dart from the car.

Peter caught her arm. "Nothing has happened to your horse. I want to know generally what people do."

Fanning her face, Gladys replied, "Most around here have the fallen stock men out from the hunt to take the carcass away. Some send them off to Potters to get the meat money, and a few very sentimental ones hire a JCB and bury them on their land. That's probably what I'll do this time. The others have gone to the hunt, but Cara is special."

"Would you know who in the last few years has buried their horse?"

Gladys frowned. "Off-hand I don't. It's not something I really dwell on."

Releasing her arm, Peter said, "Could you ring me if anyone comes to mind in the next few hours?"

With a wave, Gladys agreed to have a think and skipped down the path to join Dick who was waiting for her in the doorway. Once she vacated the car, Fiona slid across to the front passenger seat. Peter joined her but didn't start the engine as she expected. Instead, he rang DS Ward and asked for an update. As soon as he finished that call he made another.

"Shouldn't we be getting out to the farmhouse?" Fiona said.

Peter raised a hand to silence her. "Dr Carney? I'm calling about the young lady you saw earlier today… Yes, yes, DI Williams passed that on to me… We understand Ellen was convinced someone was trying to take her substitute baby from her… did she give a name or any reasoning for her paranoia? … Thanks for your time. You've been most helpful."

"Did he give you a name?" Fiona asked.

"No. I was being polite about the extent of his helpfulness."

"Are we going out to Park Farm now?" Fiona asked.

"No," Peter replied, still not starting the car. "If Gladys' timing is correct, Creer left the cottage nearly three hours ago. Assuming he's not stupid, he has realised the farm is being watched. If he doubled back to the cottage, he would have seen our vehicles outside."

"So where would he go?"

"He's going to do one of two things: cut his losses and leave the country or try to recover his money tonight. Ring the station and see if they've discovered who rents or owns the cottage."

While Fiona was on the phone, Peter picked up her laptop and scrolled through the notes she'd made on Ellen. "Interesting," he said out loud, distracting Fiona briefly.

He drummed his fingers impatiently on the steering wheel before starting the car.

"They'll get back to me as they find out," Fiona said, slipping her phone into her pocket. "One odd thing that's occurred to me. Lucy Bassett said only family knew about Ellen's pregnancy, so how did Creer find out?"

Fiona wriggled to retrieve her ringing phone while fastening her seat belt. Peter turned the car around at speed, causing her to bang her shoulder against the door frame. She looked crossly at Peter who ignored her as he accelerated.

"Brilliant. Thanks," she said into the phone before asking Peter, "What's the rush?"

"Who rented the house?" Peter asked.

"Jane Salt owns it. It was left to her by her grandparents, although she has never lived there. She kept it rented out until a few months ago when she gave her tenants notice of her intention to sell it. It has been empty ever since."

"He's a player. Using all these women. Gaining their trust knowing he was going to discard them all. Question is, were any of them any different? I'm assuming they were all promised they'd be sharing an affluent future with him and yet there was only one woman who knew the location of his ill-gotten gains."

"Yes, Ellen. Is that where we're headed? She's staying with her aunt out of the way of things."

"That's where we're headed, but no, not Ellen."

"Not her mother, surely?"

"I haven't completely discounted that possibility, but she's my second choice. I guess we'll know when we get there," Peter said.

"You mean Kathy?"

"Once we accept Ellen didn't hide the key inside the doll, who else could have done it?"

"Why didn't she just keep the key hidden herself?" Fiona asked.

"I guess she couldn't risk anyone finding the key in her possession and discovering her relationship with Creer. Once it became clear Ellen was never going to let the doll out of her sight, where better a place to hide it? It may have even been a spur of the moment thing to start with. The police and media didn't leave the family alone for months. Maybe she had it in her possession when there was a surprise visit from the police, and she panicked?" Peter suggested.

Keeping his eyes focused on the road he said, "The key itself is possibly not essential. The money has been buried in a safe with a horse. I've just found out from your interview notes that Kathy lost a horse that was very special to her at about the right time."

"But Kathy doesn't have her own land. Surely her little garden wouldn't be big enough?"

"Possibly she persuaded the farmer who owned the land where she kept her horse? If she was prepared to pay, I don't suppose many farmers would turn down a tearful request for a hole to be dug." Peter said.

Pulling up outside the rank of cottages they found Kathy's home in darkness with the front door wide open. Peter climbed out of the car and said, "I've a feeling we might be too late. Ring the station and get checks at the airports and ferries while I go and see."

TWENTY-EIGHT

Climbing the steep stone steps to the terraced cottage, he could hear hysterical sobbing coming from inside. He crept inside through the open door. Lucy Bassett was lying awkwardly in the narrow hallway. He knelt by her side while working out which room the sobs were coming from. Lucy was alive but unconscious, and he decided she could wait.

He stood to the side and slowly opened the door to a small living room. Ellen rocked forwards and backwards hugging her bundle of rags that were torn. She clutched the stuffing from the soft doll, wet from her tears, in one hand and held it to her face. She gave a pitiful cry as Peter approached. "The animals ripped her heart out."

Fiona entered the room behind Peter. "An ambulance is on its way, and they won't be able to leave the country on their passports."

"Is Lucy still unconscious?" Peter asked, before crouching next to Ellen.

"Get away. Get away," Ellen screeched hysterically.

Peter stood and backed away. "It's okay. I don't want to harm either of you. I just wanted to ask you some questions about what happened here."

Ellen raised her head and screamed, holding the high note for an impossibly long time. Her eyes bulged as her face turned a deep crimson.

Peter walked Fiona to the door. "Can you try with her? Find

out how long ago they left and whether she knows where Kathy buried that horse of hers. I'll wait with her mother out in the hallway."

Lucy's condition remained the same. Peter sat next to her with his back resting against the wall, listening to her even breathing. He jumped up when the sound of sirens announced the ambulance's arrival. Meeting the paramedics at the door, he was relieved to see one of them was female. He led them to Lucy while explaining Ellen's issues with men.

Fiona joined him in the hallway. "Sorry. I couldn't get anything from her."

They were pushed from the hallway into the kitchen to allow the paramedics to manoeuvre their stretcher into place. Peter noticed one of the two mugs on the table was still half full. Feeling the mug, he said, "It's still lukewarm, so we must have just missed them."

"We didn't pass a car on the road, and Kathy's mini isn't outside. They must have gone in the opposite direction," Fiona said.

"You'd better contact the hospital and let Ian Bassett know about his wife's and daughter's condition. I assume they'll be taking them to Birstall General. Christ knows what they'll do with Ellen without a parent around to look after her. As he's now conscious, try to get someone to ask him if he knows where Kathy's horse was buried. Failing that, where it was kept beforehand."

Peter rang Gladys, "Hi Gladys, do you know Kathy Hooper? ... You do. Brilliant. Do you know where she kept her horse or where it was buried? ... Thanks. Ring me back on this number."

Listening to Fiona's side of the conversation, it was obvious the hospital in Birmingham weren't being very cooperative. Once she slipped her phone into her pocket, he said, "Gladys is going to ring me back. She has a friend who might know where the horse was buried."

From the kitchen, they heard the clang of the stretcher trolley as they wheeled Lucy out to the waiting ambulance. Coming out of the kitchen, they saw Ellen huddled in a blanket being helped to walk behind the trolley. Peter answered his phone as Ellen disappeared from sight through the front door. "We've got an address. You'll never guess where."

"Surprise me," Fiona said, following him from the house.

"James Palmer's farm. Fingers crossed he's in, and he knows where on his property it was buried. From memory, his farm covered a fair bit of land."

On the way, the wind picked up, buffeting the side of the car. They drove across the undulating switch back lane surrounded by open farmland which had been the cause of so much misery in the past. As they turned to follow the steep incline down to the more sheltered position of the farmhouse, a loud crack of thunder preceded a hailstorm. By the time they arrived at the electronic gates to the farmyard, a pile of hailstones covered the car bonnet. The gate swung open on their approach, and they drove in past a newly built garage and parked alongside the house. Freezing rain tore at them as they ran up the wheelchair ramp and across the raised stone patio. James threw open the front door and met them as old friends, ushering them into the tight space of the porch out of the rain.

Handing them both heavy wax jackets, James said, "Here, put these on. It's bitterly cold out there and only going to get colder."

Gratefully putting the coats on over their existing jackets, Peter said, "I can't remember the last time I saw the sun. Just grey, grey and more grey."

"You're not wrong there," James said jovially. Pulling on a pair of wellingtons, he shouted down the hallway, "I'm off to show them where Kathy's horse was buried. I won't be long."

Pulling a cloth cap over his head, he said, "Follow me," and started to run down the ramp and towards the row of open barns behind the house. Once they reached the barn, he added, "With it being so wet, the only way we're going to get there is in a tractor. Unless you want to get on the quad bike behind me and get drenched, that is. Even the truck would struggle to get there the ground is so saturated and churned up." He climbed the steep step to the tractor cab and pulled down a temporary seat. "It will be a tight squeeze, and you'll have to share. Once you pull the door shut behind you, it'll hold you in place."

The tractor started up and moved away with far less noise than Peter expected. Wedged between Fiona and the door, he twisted sideways to face James. "Are you saying the location isn't accessible with a standard vehicle, not even a four-wheel drive?"

"Not all the way at this time of year. If someone tried to go up there by car today, they'd get stuck on the incline. No one local would be stupid enough to attempt it." He was interrupted by another clap of thunder, and a streak of lightning lit up the countryside. "Not a good night for man or beast to be out. You said on the phone it was urgent you see the spot tonight. How come?"

Peter and Fiona exchanged a hopeful look. It seemed the atrocious weather was going to be a help for once. Peter was flung on top of Fiona as the tractor turned off the lane and bounced along the edge of a muddy field. It took Peter several attempts to right himself as the tractor lurched over the uneven ground. He pulled out his phone and asked James, "Can you give us a rough estimate of where we're headed? The nearest point to an actual road a standard vehicle could reach would be great."

James tipped his cloth cap back and scratched his head. "Depends which direction they come from, I guess."

"From the village of Alderston."

"If they haven't come this way across my land, I reckon Old Gloucester Road by Mistress Cottage. Yup. That would be my best bet."

"Which is where?" Peter asked.

"About half a mile down from the Supworth crossroads." Nodding towards the phone in Peter's hand he said in a loud voice, "To get on Old Gloucester, tell them to take the right fork after The Bear and Ragged Staff Inn on their left. A short distance along there, before the crossroads, is the old Wiltshire Path which joins the road proper from behind Mistress Cottage. They can't miss it. It's the only house on that stretch of road. That's the closest they'll get in cars."

"Got that?" Peter said, into his phone before slipping it back into his pocket.

The gloom gave way to darkness as they trundled along at a much slower pace. Peter held on to the handle above the door to prevent himself from being thrown into the front of the cab by the tractor's motion. James shook his head and chuckled to himself. After they'd covered the length of the field, the tractor tipped back as it started its ascent up a steep incline.

James patted the centre of the steering wheel and said, "Don't worry yourselves. This is what this little beauty was built to do, and I know every inch of my land." After a short distance, James half stood and looked over the front of the tractor at the ground lit by the beam of the headlights. "Well, how about that. It seems someone else has been this way this evening," he said, pointing out deep fresh tractor tracks.

Holding tight to the handle with his left hand and leaning against the front windscreen with his right, Peter risked half standing to peer at the rising ground beneath them. "How recently do you think?"

"As they're only half filled with rain water I'd say an hour ago, tops. Probably more like half an hour ago." James peered over the front of the cab again and rubbed his chin. "You know, I reckon they're from a digger, not a tractor. Why the hell would someone want to dig up a dead horse in this weather?"

This time Peter and Fiona shared a worried look.

"Hold on tight now. Here's where it gets really steep." Peter and Fiona were unable to fight gravity and felt pinned to the seat as the tractor tipped back and slowly ground its way up the steep bank. Clumps of mud clung to the tractor, and the windscreen wipers worked overtime, sloshing brown rivulets of running water as the rain turned to sleet.

There was a slight sway from behind as the tractor reached the apex before the front wheels found solid ground. James exclaimed, "Well I'll be," as the tractor levelled out and the lights illuminated a battered old yellow digger. "That's Ian Bassett's digger. What's that daft old bugger doing up here?"

The two occupants of the digger turned around in the cab to face them, their faces hidden by the mud-smeared windows despite the bright glare from the tractor lights. Peter reached for the tractor door handle. James reached across and pulled the door shut as the digger reversed at speed towards them. James accelerated forwards as quickly as possible, but Peter and Fiona were flung across the cab as the digger caught them a glancing blow.

"Damn, they're getting away," Fiona said, pushing the weight of Peter from her.

James turned the tractor around. "Not a chance. That old digger can go thirty at most on a good solid surface. This little beauty will catch it up with ease."

"Unless they're headed for wherever they parked their car," Peter said. "Powerful though it may be, a tractor isn't going to keep up with a car."

Fiona gripped the bar on the front of the cab with both hands, bracing herself against gravity. Her knuckles turned white as the tractor plunged down the steep incline they'd just climbed. The lights from the digger and the tractor bounced wildly on the rough terrain.

"Depends how quick your friends are. They're definitely heading towards Wiltshire Path. I'll try to cut them off before they reach the lane." James steered hard to the right, causing Fiona to fall across Peter's lap. "Sorry, it's going to get a bit bumpy here, but he'll have to turn at some point as well. By taking the rougher ground he's avoiding, I might just be able to get in front of him."

Peter pulled out his phone to give an update while trying to remain upright as the seat he shared with Fiona bounced up and down like a space hopper. At one point, Peter rose half a foot from the seat and banged the top of his head on the roof of the cab. He gave up with the phone and joined Fiona in gripping the bar that ran along the front of the cab with both hands. "This has got to be the first police chase in a tractor!"

James grinned across at them. "Best fun I've had in ages."

The tractor hit another ridge in the ground, bouncing Peter

and Fiona from the seat. "Just watch where you're going!" Peter shouted, pulling himself up from the footwell.

Clinging onto the bar, Fiona said, "Why are we driving so far away from him? He's getting away from us by driving straight down the hill."

"I'm going to cut him off when he has to turn right," James shouted back.

"But he's not turning right," Peter shouted.

"He's not, is he? That can't be Ian driving then. He's not that daft," James said and slowed the tractor, bringing it to a halt.

"What are you doing? Why have we stopped?" Peter and Fiona shouted in unison.

James grinned and then chuckled. He leaned back in his seat and, nodding towards the digger, said, "This is going to be hysterical. Three. Two. One."

On the count of one, the digger lights swung violently to the right before disappearing completely into the ground. Through the mist and rain, they could just make out the flashing orange light on the top of the cab as the digger came to a sudden halt.

James slowly turned the tractor towards the digger, laughing all the time. "That's going to be a hell of a job to get out. I'll have to have a good think about how much I'm going to charge Bassett to recover his digger."

Peter peered through the windscreen. "Just get us over there, will you. You can concentrate on the financial implications later."

Laughing to himself, James accelerated.

"Look," Fiona shouted, pointing towards the digger.

"They're going to make a run for it." Peter again reached for the door handle.

"Don't be stupid, man," James said, stopping him. "They're stuck in a river, and that water will be freezing." James turned the tractor hard right and added, "The bridge is only a short distance away. We'll catch them up well before they reach the lane which is probably where they're headed. That's if they know where they're going. Anyone local would know the river runs through here even if they weren't exactly sure where the bridges are."

Peter and Fiona strained to keep their eyes on the two running figures as the tractor slowly trundled over a narrow bridge before turning left and accelerating across the field. The powerful headlights picked out the two running figures quite quickly.

"What do you want me to do?" James asked. "Drive past them and circle around them?"

"If you could, that would be brilliant. I'll jump down as we get closer. You may as well stay in the cab, Fiona, in case they decide to run in opposite directions."

The tractor was bearing down on the two runners when the sound of sirens could be heard in the distance. Shortly after, flashes of light could be seen passing through the trees. With a look at the rain lashing down and the bedraggled and clearly tiring runners, Peter said, "On second thoughts, I don't want to get wet unnecessarily. Try and herd them towards the lane and the officers who are on their way. We'll only jump out if one or both of them tries to double back."

Once the police cars with sirens blazing came into sight, Kathy tried to make an about turn and fell face down in the mud where she remained. Creer, realising he was trapped, came to a halt and raised his hands above his head.

As they were giving themselves up without a fight, Peter stayed in the tractor cab. He jumped down and wandered over only when the pair were captured and sat dripping mud in the back seat of two separate cars. "Take them back to the station and get them cleaned up. I'll be there later to get their statements."

Climbing back into the tractor, he said to James, "Do you want to make some money tonight?"

"Sure."

"The site up there needs to be secured and what we believe is a safe recovered. Are you happy to ferry officers and equipment up there?"

"I wouldn't miss it for the world," James replied.

TWENTY-NINE

Losing his nest egg had aged Creer overnight. To everyone's surprise, when the safe was recovered, it was found to be empty. He appeared depressed but quietly agreed to give them a full statement before he was returned to Shoreham Prison to await his fate. He confirmed much of what they already knew. He had used Jane to help him escape. It had been Kathy's idea to persuade Jane to try to recover the key. When she failed to gain access by posing as a journalist, she'd asked Vivien Morse to steal the doll from Ellen. By using the social workers, Kathy hoped to divert any suspicion away from her. Creer was quite insistent he knew nothing about Vivien's murder.

Despite going over and over the same ground, he insisted he had no knowledge of how Jane had ended up dead in the cottage with him. He accepted the obvious conclusion he must have killed her and to some extent seemed resigned to the assumption as he couldn't give any alternative explanation of what had happened. His medical records confirmed he had suffered blackouts before, but he refused to confess to a murder, he wasn't aware he'd committed.

During the final interview, he seemed in a better frame of mind. With a boyish grin, he said, "The matter will rest in the minds of the jury. I had no idea how the couple in Birmingham ended up dead, but I was still convicted of their murder. If it doesn't go my way again this time, then life inside isn't too bad. Plenty of activities and three cooked meals a day. I might even do one of those Open University courses and get some letters after my name. At least I won't have to survive on a British pension."

Kathy Hooper was even more frustrating. On the advice of her solicitors, she replied, "No comment," to most of their questions. She only admitted to hiding a safe for Creer and agreeing under duress to show him where it was buried. Her claim she had no idea what it contained and had never looked inside was met with raised eyebrows, but she stubbornly stuck to her story.

After hearing the same story for the third time, Peter closed his file abruptly and left the room without warning. Fiona formally brought the interview to a close before following Peter from the room. She found him in the corridor looking relaxed and cheerful, chatting to Sykes, the front desk sergeant. "Everything okay?" she asked.

Peter grimaced. "Sorry, I've developed a distinct dislike of that woman and didn't see the point of sitting through another hour of her lies."

"Why don't we just charge her and let her go? No jury is going to believe she had no idea what she was hiding. She'll be convicted of aiding and abetting without a doubt on what we already have."

"Release her? Do you really think we'll find her again?"

"Where would she go?"

"Anywhere she liked, with the money she took from the safe," Peter replied. "It has probably been invested in an off-shore account somewhere. Come on. We've work to do. I'm determined to charge someone with the murder of Vivien, and this is far from over."

Almost running to keep up, Fiona said, "Sorry, you've lost me. What are you suggesting?"

"Have you read through the initial reports on Creer's previous crime spree? They all indicate the investigating officers were convinced Creer wasn't working alone. They dropped the charges against Ellen due to her age, her injuries and the fact they could only find circumstantial evidence against her. She may have been nothing but a pawn like Jane Salt all along, and it was Kathy that Creer really came down here to see. His relationship with Ellen was nothing more than a convenient cover. We need to find out where Kathy invested the money. Someone killed Vivien Morse, and it couldn't have been Creer."

"It couldn't have been Kathy either. There's a whole host of wealthy landowners prepared to say she didn't leave the hall where her fundraiser was held from three o'clock onwards. At the time of the attack, she was in company blowing up balloons and hanging streamers. I watched her face when she was told the safe was empty. If that reaction was faked, she should be in Hollywood."

"Invite her to join your drama group," Peter said dismissively.

"I'm convinced the look of shock and anger she gave was totally genuine. She may have been killing time here waiting for Creer's release, but that's the only killing she's done," Fiona said.

Peter stopped in his tracks. "You could be right, but I still want a full check on her finances," he said, before marching towards the car park.

Outside the car, Fiona said, "Where are we going anyway?"

"We were heading for Kathy's house."

"And now?" Fiona asked, easing herself into the passenger seat.

Peter thought for a while before decisively pulling the seat belt across himself. "The Horseshoe Inn. I need to think."

A real fire burned in the corner of the near empty bar. Neville welcomed them from his bar stool. For the first time ever, Lorraine was not dashing around with food orders but was sitting next to her husband, looking glum.

"Quiet in here today," Peter commented.

"Tell us about it. This awful weather is keeping everyone away. Last night Andi was the only customer in here at eight o'clock. In fact, it was so dead the dogs were our second-best customers of the day," Lorraine said.

"Cheer up, dear, or you'll scare everyone away," Neville said. "It'll pick up in a week or so. Relax and enjoy the lull." Smiling at Fiona and Peter, he added, "Can't sit still, that one. What would you both like?"

Lorraine disappeared through the doorway behind the bar in a huff only to reappear a short while later wearing a coat. "I'm off for some retail therapy. I'll try not to spend the entire week's takings in less than an hour."

Neville kept them chatting at the bar. When the pub phone rang, Peter collected their drinks and moved to a table tucked in the corner near the fire. Once settled he asked, "Is everything okay at home?"

Surprised, Fiona replied, "Yes, why do you ask?"

Peter shrugged. "We didn't finish until the early hours this morning. I got grief from Sally for waking her up when I got in. I just wondered how you fared?"

Not satisfied with the answer, Fiona gave Peter a prolonged look over the rim of her glass as she sipped her water. Placing it carefully on a beer mat, she said, "You've never shown any concern before about what time we finish. What's changed?"

"Abbie Ward made a comment the other day."

"Abbie should mind her own business."

"She was concerned. Forget I said anything. It was clumsy of me, and I would like to think if there was anything wrong, you would tell me." Peter held eye contact, trying to read her expression and willing her to speak.

Fiona broke the eye connection. "Everything is fine. I thought we came here to think about the case and establish who could have killed Vivien."

They drank in silence, staring at the flames in the open fire before Peter said, "What do you think of Creer's claim he has no recollection of killing Jane Salt? He said the same thing at his trial about the couple murdered in the botched burglary."

"Absolute tosh," Fiona replied.

"I thought you would say that. If you didn't, we would also have to consider who did kill her and the most obvious culprit would be Kathy in a jealous rage. If Kathy killed Jane, then maybe she killed Vivien as well."

"Why are you so sure Jane didn't kill Vivien? The time between their meeting in the pub and her death is very short. Four hours, absolute maximum."

"I'm not. I'm balancing your dislike of Jane with mine of Kathy. The only problem is both women have airtight alibis for the likely time of Vivien's attack. Alibis given by reliable people with nothing to gain by misleading us. Unless, of course, their alibis were bought? Whoever beat us to the contents of the safe is by all accounts now very wealthy," Peter said.

"So, we go back and re-interview everyone who confirmed Kathy was organising a cocktail party to raise funds for an injured jockey. Then we challenge Sheila Bond about the alibi she gave Jane."

"What are you suggesting? At some point, one of them slipped away unnoticed into a phone kiosk for a quick change of clothes? Then drove out to meet Vivien in the rain in the middle of the woods and returned looking immaculate without anyone noticing?" Peter said.

"It's not unusual for someone to have to rush off just before an event. There's always something overlooked until the last minute," Fiona said.

"According to the witnesses, Kathy had everything under control and didn't leave the hall. As Jane was sharing a meal for two, her absence would have been even more obvious. Unless you want to call a bunch of titled ladies and a High Court Judge liars, neither of them could have killed Vivien." Peter drained his mug of Old Peculiar and stared morosely into the fireplace. "I have this little voice in my head saying something doesn't fit in with what we've been told, but I can't put my finger on what it is. It's staring us in the face, and yet I can't see it, for the life of me."

"That happens to me all the time. It's an age thing," Neville said, placing fresh drinks on the table. "On the house. May I join you?"

Hiding his frustration at the intrusion, Peter pushed out a stool that had been tucked under the table. "Please do. Maybe we need a distraction."

"I often find that is the case. Moments of inspiration come to me when I least expect it," Neville said.

They made small talk about the pub trade until the door

opened and a man entered looking uncomfortable in an ill-fitting suit.

"Matt, come and join us," Neville said. "You haven't been in for weeks and what's with the suit?"

"Don't know why I bothered putting it on just to hear my damn solicitor confirm I can barely live on the income she's left me. And he charged me an arm and a leg for the information." Matt sat down next to Neville. "I'll be telling my son when he's older never to get married. But if he does, never ever get divorced. The bitch gets the house, the bulk of my income and even a share of my pension. I'm going to be a pauper begging on the streets just to keep her in the style she's accustomed to, while she sits on her fat arse all day doing nothing."

Neville stood with his hand on Matt's shoulder. "I'll get you a pint."

"Thanks," Matt replied. He looked up at Peter and Fiona. "Sorry to interrupt you guys. It's been a bad day. The ex is totally clearing me out. I would have been better off if I had hired a top hit man and buried her seven feet deep in the garden where no one would ever find her."

Peter jumped up. "That's it!"

"Sorry, mate, I didn't want to upset you and the missus. I was just venting."

Neville looked on, confused, holding the pint mug as Peter clapped his hands on Matt's cheeks. "You little beauty." Grabbing his jacket from the back of his chair he said to Fiona, "Come on. I've cracked it."

Fiona shrugged an apology to Matt and said, "Cracked what?"

"The sudden change in behaviour."

THIRTY

Holding tight to the door handle as Peter sped through the country lanes, Fiona asked, "Where are we going?"

"Sorry, you were right. I should have taken more notice at the time of the expensive clothes he was buying when he had a reputation of keeping moths in his wallet. Nigel Morse has the contents of the safe. Vivian Morse was killed by her husband."

"Whoa, hang on. As far as we know, only Kathy knew about the location of the buried safe. How on earth would Nigel Morse discover it even existed, let alone where to find it?" Fiona asked.

"Living in the same house, he must have known Vivien received letters from Creer on a regular basis. Don't forget he was bitter and probably obsessive about the whole issue. It was Nigel who broke into the houses looking for the correspondence, not Dick. Think back to when we first visited him. The letter on the kitchen cabinet he quickly put in his pocket saying it was from his mother." Peter said.

"Of course. By the time we discovered the letter writing, Nigel Morse had already been eliminated as a major suspect, so the connection was never made. And he took Vivien's dog with him, so its barking wouldn't alert the neighbours, he was out for the evening," Fiona said.

"And he made that vague comment about lonely inmates telling the same hard luck stories to anyone gullible enough to believe them."

"The drunken night he spent with Kathy! When she passed out

drunk, he snooped around and came across a bundle of letters with the same handwriting. He must have read them and discovered all about the safe and where it was buried," Fiona said.

"It wouldn't surprise me if he stalked Vivien on an evening. Or maybe he drove around the area looking for a landmark mentioned in the letters and happened to see Vivien that evening by chance. If you've argued with a friend and stormed off, what do you sometimes do next to calm yourself down?"

"Go for a run usually," Fiona replied.

"Dressed in high heels that might be difficult. But you might stop your car and walk a short distance to vent." Peter pulled onto the dual carriageway that bypassed the small villages. "I don't want to pre-warn him we're on our way in case he runs, but we have no idea whether he's at work, on the road or at home. At the next roundabout should I turn left towards Sapperton or right towards Birstall? Your shout."

"Pull over. I've a better idea." Fiona spoke into her phone. "Hello, Playthings? I'm the owner of The Entertainer toy shop in Exeter. Could I speak to your Mr Morse please concerning my last order...No it's an ongoing issue. I really need to speak to Mr Morse directly...He knows all about the account, and I don't want to go through it all again with someone else ... Oh. Well, I'll just have to wait until he returns. I don't suppose you know what time his flight is? Maybe I could have a quick word before he leaves ... Never mind. Thank you for your help." Fiona slipped her phone into her pocket and said, "Left towards Sapperton. And you'd better get your foot down if you want to catch him before he leaves. Otherwise, we'll have to drive out to Birstall airport."

"Where's he headed?"

"According to his employers, Copenhagen for a major toy fair. His flight isn't due for another three hours, so he should be at home."

Approaching Morse's house, Fiona said, "They did a pretty good search of the house and car before. Why do you think they didn't find anything?"

"Just goes to show you can't rely too heavily on technology. Our jobs are still safe from computers for a few years yet."

"It's still a worry if they missed important evidence."

"Maybe he isn't as stupid as he looks and realised we'd be looking at him as a prime suspect. With Creer's money safely banked somewhere, buying a car and a set of clothes solely for his snooping about and disposing of them afterwards would represent a minor investment," Peter said.

"Why kill her? He could have taken the money and disappeared without anyone being any the wiser."

"He knew she'd not let it go and chase him for the divorce settlement? Jealousy and anger? I'm guessing the letters that passed between his wife and Creer would have been intimate and possibly steamy. Maybe he felt she'd mocked him and needed to be punished?" Peter suggested.

Peter parked his car in front of Nigel Morse's BMW, blocking it in should he attempt to leave. "His car is here, so hopefully he is too, and you can ask him to answer that question."

Nigel Morse opened his door on their first knock. With a forced smile, he said, "Thank you for arresting my wife's murderer. I heard it on the radio this morning.
Unfortunately, I can't talk now because I need to leave to catch a plane."

"Oh, where are you going?" Peter asked.

"Copenhagen for a toy fair. I do need to leave quite sharpish."

"What time is your flight?" Fiona asked.

A bead of sweat ran down the side of Nigel's face. "In less than two hours. My boss won't be happy if I'm not on that flight."

"I've some good news for you. You've got the time wrong. The next flight out of Birstall heading for Copenhagen is in three hours, so it seems we do have time for a quick chat before you leave," Peter said. "Can we come in?"

Reluctantly Nigel opened the door wider to let them pass. "It'll have to be quick."

Lined up on the floor taking up much of the narrow kitchen were four large suitcases. Stepping over them Peter said, "You're taking a lot of luggage. How long are you staying?"

"Only a couple of nights but the suitcases contain samples. They take up a lot of space."

With insufficient room for her to move past them, Fiona bent to inspect the suitcases. "They're all locked."

"Yes. That's because they are samples of our new range. They're not available yet so we wouldn't want an industry spy to gain access before I showcase them at the fair," Nige explained.

"Is that so?" Peter said, maintaining his friendly smile. "The soft toy market must be very competitive. Who would have thought competitors would spy on sales reps and try to get access to the samples. It's a crazy world we live in."

Sweat was pouring from Nigel's face as he became increasingly agitated. "Yes. Crazy, crazy world."

"Are you feeling okay?" Fiona asked. "You look very flushed. Could I get you a glass of water?"

"I'm fine, thank you. Just a little nervous about catching my plane on time. If you must know, I'm a nervous flyer. I do want to arrive at the airport early, so I can try to relax before boarding. What is it you want to know?"

"Could you open the suitcases for us? Then we'll be on our way," Peter said.

Leaning against the kitchen counter trying to strike a casual pose but failing badly, Nigel said, "I'd love to, but I'm afraid I can't. Company standards. I don't have access to the contents. Someone will meet me in Copenhagen with the keys."

Peter burst out laughing. "You've a wonderful imagination, I'll give you that."

"It's the truth."

"And the airline will accept four locked suitcases without question in this day and age? Why don't you try one of the keys you're wearing around your neck on a chain? You never know. You might get lucky," Peter said.

Nigel launched himself towards Peter, pushing him backwards into Fiona and made a dash for the back door. Managing to remain upright despite tripping over the suitcases, Peter quickly rebalanced himself and ran after Nigel, grabbing him by the scruff of the neck at the door. He bent his arm behind his back and turned him back towards the kitchen. With his free hand, he pulled the chain from around Nigel's neck. He frogmarched him back into the kitchen and threw the set of keys to Fiona. "Open them."

Fiona opened each in turn and felt all around inside under neatly packed clothes. "Nothing," she finally said after a thorough inspection of the fourth case.

"I told you," Nigel said. "You've seen inside my cases so can you please release me."

"Strange, I haven't found any samples." Fiona held up the chain of keys. "But there is still one key I haven't used."

"Go and check the rest of the house for another case," Peter said.

After a short while, Fiona returned triumphantly with a locked briefcase. She set it on the kitchen countertop, unlocked it and flipped the two catches. She gave a passport a cursory glance before discarding it on the side. Next, she looked through a wad of travel documents. "Oh dear. It seems your company has made a dreadful mistake. These flight tickets are for Zurich." She felt to the bottom of the case and retrieved a large brown envelope. Making a space on the countertop, she tipped the contents out. Flicking through the paperwork, she announced, "Goodness, Nigel, you are a wealthy man. With this amount of money in a Swiss bank account, why do you work for a toy firm? I'd be sipping champagne on the Riviera if this were my bank account."

"Nigel Morse, I'm arresting you for the murder of your wife." Pulling out a pair of handcuffs from his jacket pocket, Peter said, "Tell him the rest of it, DI Williams."

THIRTY-ONE

With a contented smile, Peter signed off the last document on his desk and threw his plastic coffee cup across the room towards the bin. He thumped the air in celebration of his direct hit. "Get in there, my son."

Looking across at Fiona, he added, "You done? I think it's time for a proper drink. Joining me?"

Fiona grinned and collected her jacket hanging on the other side of the room.

"Happy with The Horseshoe or would you prefer to walk to The Squire?" Peter asked.

"The Squire would be better," Fiona replied.

Peter shouted, "Leave it," when the phone rang.

Fiona mouthed, "Sorry, too late," as she lifted the receiver. "Okay, we'll be down in a minute."

From the doorway, Peter said, "That had better not be work. Can't someone else deal with it?"

Walking into the corridor, Fiona replied, "It was Gladys. She's downstairs with Dick, and they've asked for us personally."

"I'm still trying to think what I can charge Dick with," Peter grumbled. "Wasting police time, mostly. The guy is a buffoon and the reason chocolate manufacturers have to say a walnut whip may contain nuts."

A beaming Gladys met them in the reception area. "I wanted you to be the first to know. Dick has asked me to marry him, and I've said yes. I hope you can both be with us on our special day."

Peter said to Dick, "A bit sudden, isn't it? How many wives can a Druid priest have?"

Dick looked troubled while Gladys looked at him questioningly. Thumping himself hard in the centre of his chest with a closed fist, Dick said, "I want you to know I've always been an honourable man. With Gladys by my side, I will never wander from the path of honesty and virtue again, and I can assure you of my good intentions to this wonderful lady you see before you. I accept any ill feelings you have towards me are my own doing, but I know how much it would mean to my betrothed if you could attend our nuptials."

"Ignore him, Dick," Fiona said, lightly cuffing Peter around the head. "Congratulations. We'd both love to attend."

Thank you for reading my book. I hope you enjoyed reading it as much as I enjoyed writing it.

◆ ◆ ◆

The Peter Hatherall series

The Skeletons of Birkbury
Bells on her Toes
Point of No Return
Who Killed Vivien Morse?
Twisted Truth
The Paperboy

The Trouble series

Trouble at Clenchers Mill
Trouble at Fatting House

Stand-alone novels

Fool Me Once
Debts & Druids

BOOKS IN THIS SERIES

Peter Hatherall Mystery

The Skeletons Of Birkbury

Bells On Her Toes

Point Of No Return

Who Killed Vivien Morse?

Twisted Truth

The Paperboy

BOOKS BY THIS AUTHOR

A Fiery End

Trouble At Clenchers Mill

Trouble At Fatting House

Fool Me Once

Debts & Druids